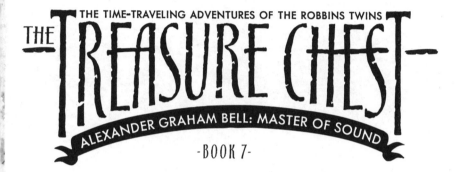

THE TIME-TRAVELING ADVENTURES OF THE ROBBINS TWINS

THE TREASURE CHEST

ALEXANDER GRAHAM BELL: MASTER OF SOUND

-BOOK 7-

BY *NEW YORK TIMES* BEST-SELLING AUTHOR

ANN HOOD

Grosset & Dunlap
An Imprint of Penguin Group (USA)

In memory of Barbara Bejoian

GROSSET & DUNLAP
Published by the Penguin Group
Penguin Group (USA), 375 Hudson Street, New York, New York 10014, USA

USA | Canada | UK | Ireland | Australia | New Zealand | India | South Africa | China
Penguin Books Ltd, Registered Offices: 80 Strand, London WC2R 0RL, England

For more information about the Penguin Group visit penguin.com

Text © 2013 by Ann Hood. Art © 2013 by Denis Zilber. Published by Grosset & Dunlap, a division of Penguin Young Readers Group,
345 Hudson Street, New York, New York 10014. GROSSET & DUNLAP is a trademark of Penguin Group (USA). Printed in the U.S.A.

Library of Congress Cataloging-in-Publication Data is available.

Design by Giuseppe Castellano.
Map illustration by Giuseppe Castellano and © 2013 by Penguin Group (USA).

ISBN 978-0-448-45730-7 (pbk)   10 9 8 7 6 5 4 3 2 1
ISBN 978-0-448-45740-6 (hc)   10 9 8 7 6 5 4 3 2 1

ALWAYS LEARNING   PEARSON

CHAPTER 1

LOVEBIRDS

"Married!" Maisie and Felix's mother shrieked in disbelief. Her blue eyes widened as she surveyed Great-Uncle Thorne and Penelope Merriweather grinning at her like teenagers in love.

Maisie, Felix, and their mother were in the Dining Room eating dinner—the bacon-and-egg spaghetti they loved so much—when Great-Uncle Thorne and Penelope burst in shouting their news. That is, Great-Uncle Thorne burst in. Penelope followed, walking slowly with her short, mincing steps

Maisie and Felix sneaked glances at each other. They had only been back from their visit with their father in New York City for a few hours and had not yet broached the subject of *him* getting married.

Great-Uncle Thorne lifted Penelope's hand to show off a diamond so big that it looked like a fake one from a bubble-gum machine.

"Is that real?" Maisie gasped.

"Of course it's real," Great-Uncle Thorne said, stiffening. "It belonged to my mother, Ariane. It's the Pickworth diamond."

"But why in the world would you get married at your age?" their mother said, her voice rising with each syllable.

"Why?" Great-Uncle Thorne roared. "Because we're in love! Isn't that what lovebirds do? Get married—"

"And have children?" Maisie and Felix's mother interrupted.

Maisie couldn't stifle a laugh. Great-Uncle Thorne whipped his head toward her and knit his enormous white eyebrows together.

"Don't be impertinent," he said.

Maisie made a mental note to look up that word. *Impertinent.* Although she could guess from the context what it meant.

"I haven't been married since the Depression," Penelope said with a sigh. She shook her head sadly. "He lost everything in the crash and had to be sent to a sanitarium."

"Poor bugger," Great-Uncle Thorne said.

"What crash?" Felix asked, trying to keep up.

Great-Uncle Thorne groaned. "Don't you imbeciles know *anything*?"

"The stock market crash of 1929," Penelope said. "So many people lost everything."

"Not the Pickworths!" Great-Uncle Thorne said gleefully.

"When is this wedding?" Maisie and Felix's mother asked unhappily.

"I always wanted to be a June bride," Penelope said dreamily. "Oscar and I eloped on New Year's Eve. Very romantic. I wore a lovely pale blue dress."

"But you deserve to wear a beautiful white gown and walk down the Grand Staircase—"

"You're getting married here?" their mother asked.

"My father always got married here," Great-Uncle Thorne said dismissively.

"How many times did Phinneas Pickworth get married?" Felix asked.

"Five, six . . . who can remember?" Great-Uncle Thorne said.

"I did like that aviatrix," Penelope said.

"The one Mom's room is named for?" Felix asked.

"The point is," Great-Uncle Thorne said, clearly tired of all the small talk, "we are getting married and plans must be made. We need to organize an engagement party, plan the trip to Paris—"

"Paris?" their mother said, looking more and more bewildered.

"For the wedding dress," Great-Uncle Thorne said.

He took his black leather agenda and his gold pen from his inside jacket pocket and began to scribble furiously.

"Wow," Maisie said. "Everybody's getting married."

"Maisie!" Felix hissed.

Their mother turned toward Maisie as if she was in slow motion.

"Everybody?" she said softly.

"Uh . . . Penelope and Great-Uncle Thorne and . . . ," Maisie stammered.

"And?" their mother said, waiting.

"Have you spoken to Dad lately?" Felix interjected.

"He called, but I didn't call him back," she said. She chewed her bottom lip, the way she did when she was nervous.

"Maybe we should finish dinner, and then you can call Dad back?" Felix offered.

Maisie brightened. "Great idea!"

She sat back down and dug into her spaghetti with exaggerated gusto.

"I think this is the best batch ever, Mom," she said with her mouth full.

Penelope helped herself to some. "I haven't had carbonara since I was in Rome with Mussolini," she said.

Felix and Great-Uncle Thorne sat, too, and Felix made a great show of taking more spaghetti and sprinkling Parmesan on it.

But their mother didn't sit down. She didn't even move. She just watched them all for what seemed like forever to Felix, who shoveled forkfuls of spaghetti into his mouth to avoid having to say anything more.

"Are you telling me," their mother said finally, her voice quivering, "that your father is getting married?"

Felix kept eating.

Maisie pretended to be chewing.

"Maisie? Felix?" their mother said in the tone that let them know she meant business.

"He is *not* getting married at Elm Medona," Great-Uncle Thorne said. "He is not a Pickworth."

"Answer me," their mother said.

"Did he say something about that?" Felix said to Maisie.

Maisie clutched her stomach. "I think . . . ," she began.

"Uh-oh," Felix said. His sister had the look she got right before she threw up, which she always did when she was upset.

"I think . . . ," Maisie said again, getting to her feet.

She didn't finish her sentence. Instead, she ran out of the room, their mother close behind her.

"This answers my question," their mother muttered as Maisie disappeared out the door.

⊃

Maisie and Felix's mother had planned a big homecoming for them. She'd picked them up at the train station, so happy to see them that she couldn't stop hugging them.

"I missed you guys," she kept saying.

She made bacon and egg spaghetti, even though Cook glared at her as she moved about the Kitchen.

"I rented a movie for us," she announced. "Family movie night!"

The movie was *My Fair Lady*, which Maisie and Felix used to love to watch with their parents when they were younger. The whole time she cooked the carbonara, their mother hummed the song "Wouldn't It Be Loverly" from the movie. Maisie and Felix knew that *My Fair Lady* was a play first, and that their mother had played the lead, Eliza Doolittle, the summer she'd met their father. When all four of them watched the movie, their parents always made private jokes about that summer, the kind of jokes that only needed one word to send one of them into a fit of laughter.

Now Maisie and Felix wondered if their mother would watch the movie at all.

After Maisie threw up, their mother gave her some ginger ale and a cool washcloth for her forehead. Then she went into her room and called their father. From all the way down the hall, Maisie and Felix could hear her, first yelling, then crying.

"Why did you have to open your big mouth?" Felix groaned, flopping on the bed beside his sister.

"Why didn't she call Dad back so he could tell her himself?" Maisie grumbled.

The door to Maisie's room flew open and their mother stood there, her face all blotchy and her eyes red and puffy.

"I guess there are lovebirds everywhere," she said. "I guess everyone is getting married."

"You aren't, are you?" Felix asked anxiously, imagining his mother marrying Bruce Fishbaum.

"No," she said. "I'm not."

"You're not?" Maisie said hopefully.

Their mother dropped onto the pink pouf.

"Do you feel well enough to watch the movie?" she asked Maisie.

"We don't have to watch—" Felix began.

"I want to watch the movie," their mother said. "I made a plan for your first night back home, and no one is going to mess it up. Not Thorne or . . . anyone."

"Great," Maisie said weakly.

"It is great," their mother said.

⊃

The three of them sat miserably watching *My*

Fair Lady as Henry Higgins tried to teach Eliza Doolittle how to speak proper English, all the while falling in love with her. No one made jokes. Their mother didn't sing along with Eliza. Instead, they sat in silence, munching popcorn and Twizzlers and feeling all mixed-up.

When the movie ended, they watched the credits roll, none of them moving.

"Thanks, Mom," Felix said. "What a terrific homecoming."

"I never understand why Eliza falls in love with Henry Higgins when he's so old," Maisie said.

Their mother sighed. "Who knows why people fall in love with each other?"

The television screen went dark.

"Do you like her?" their mother asked.

"Who?" Felix said, his heart sinking. He didn't want to make his mother feel worse.

"You know," she said. "Agatha."

"She's okay," Maisie said.

"Maybe . . . ," Felix began slowly. "Maybe you and Dad can get married again. Before it's too late."

His mother tousled his hair gently. "It doesn't work that way," she said.

Suddenly the overhead light flashed on and Great-Uncle Thorne walked in, tapping his walking stick as he moved.

"Plans, plans, plans!" he said happily, waving his black leather agenda at them.

He studied their faces. "Why so glum?" he asked.

Their mother shrugged.

"General malaise?" Great-Uncle Thorne asked her.

"Something like that," she said.

Maisie made a mental note to look up that word, too. *Malaise*. Unlike *impertinent*, she couldn't guess what *malaise* might mean.

"You three need to start making arrangements so that everything will go smoothly," Great-Uncle Thorne said, opening his agenda.

"Of course," their mother said agreeably. "We'll do whatever you need."

"Good, good," Great-Uncle Thorne said, flipping pages.

"When's the big day?" Felix asked him.

"June sixth. Penelope wants to be sure to be married under the sign of Gemini. Her last one was a Capricorn wedding, and we know how that turned out."

He tapped a page with his long finger.

"Ah! Here we are. The engagement party is one month from today," he said.

"How can we help?" their mother said.

The idea of making plans seemed to cheer her, Felix thought, relieved.

"Well, Jennifer," Great-Uncle Thorne said, "I think if the party is one month from today, then you can take . . . let's see . . . two weeks, yes, two weeks, to move out."

"Move out?" Maisie repeated because their mother seemed too dumbfounded to speak.

"I suppose you could move back to the servants' quarters," Great-Uncle Thorne said, flipping more pages.

"Back upstairs?" Felix said.

"Have you all gone deaf?" Great-Uncle Thorne boomed. "Obviously I need all of the rooms for the guests. And then after the wedding, Penelope will move to Elm Medona, and she certainly can't be expected to have a ragtag group of relatives living here once she becomes lady of the house, can she?"

"You're throwing us out of Elm Medona?" their mother said to Great-Uncle Thorne.

"Don't be ridiculous," he said.

Their mother smiled with relief.

"That's good," she said. "I thought you just said we needed to move out."

"I did!" Great-Uncle Thorne said, thumping his walking stick. This one had a diamond and sapphire tip that glistened in the glow of the TV. "Can't you hear correctly?"

"But—" their mother said, confused.

"I'm not throwing you out. I'm asking you to leave. Two entirely different things, Jennifer. You and your charming children have been my guests here, and now it's time for you to move on."

Great-Uncle Thorne and their mother stared at each other.

"Well," their mother said at last.

"Good," Great-Uncle Thorne said. He snapped his agenda shut. "Now, if you'll excuse me, I have so many details to attend to. Must get started."

They watched him walk across the room and out the door.

"This," their mother said, "has been a terrible day."

"I like it upstairs," Felix said truthfully.

Maisie and his mother glared at him.

"I do," he said.

"I suppose it's better than sleeping . . . on the street," Maisie said in a huff.

With that, she too walked out.

"I'm glad you're an optimist," his mother said. "Always seeing the glass half full."

Felix smiled. He almost recited the rhyme his father used to say at times like this: *The optimist and the pessimist, the difference is droll. The optimist sees the doughnut and the pessimist sees the hole.*

But then he thought better of it. This was the perfect time to just be quiet.

CHAPTER 2

SOMEONE LISTENS AT LAST

Much to Maisie and Felix Robbins's surprise, when they returned to Anne Hutchinson Middle School after spring break, two new students started class. And those new students were twins.

Felix watched as the new girl walked down the aisle, directly to Lily Goldberg's empty seat. He almost shouted for her to sit somewhere else, as if he could hold that seat for Lily, as if Lily might come back from Cleveland. But Felix knew that was ridiculous. He stared sadly as the new girl sat there trying, he thought, to look invisible.

"Class," Miss Landers said, "this is Rayne Ziff. She and her twin sister have moved here from San Francisco."

Everyone turned to stare at Rayne Ziff, impressed. San Francisco was about as far away as a place could be, an exotic city with fog and hippies and the Golden Gate Bridge. In fact, Miss Landers was asking the class what they knew about San Francisco and in reply, they were shouting these very things.

"Earthquakes!" Jim Duncan called out, and Miss Landers wrote that on the board, too.

Felix remembered how she had done this on his first day, and it made him feel wistful.

Bitsy Beal was bragging about her trip to San Francisco, where they stayed at some fancy hotel called the Mark Hopkins and ate Crab Louis and sourdough bread.

"*I*," Bitsy Beal said in her braggiest voice, "know a lot about San Francisco."

"Rayne's father is here for just a few months to teach at the Naval War College," Miss Landers said, to change the subject.

The Naval War College was on the other end of Newport, a serious-looking compound that Felix had never seen closeup; you had to be in the US Navy to get past the gate.

"Do you know Ghirardelli Square?" Bitsy Beal

was asking the new girl. "And Fisherman's Wharf?" She glanced around to be sure she was impressing everyone with her sophisticated knowledge of San Francisco.

"Well," Rayne said, "I know them but I never, like, actually went there. If I could help it," she added under her breath.

Bitsy looked at her, surprised. "Why not?"

"Because that's where all the tourists go," Rayne said.

Someone tittered.

"I think we should read a book that takes place in San Francisco," Miss Landers said, saving the day as usual. "Now let me see if I can think of one . . ."

Across the hall, Mrs. Witherspoon was introducing Hadley Ziff to Maisie's class, but she didn't let Hadley sit down. Instead, she made Hadley stand in front of the class and tell them where she was from and why they had moved here.

Maisie studied Hadley carefully as she talked about San Francisco and the Naval War College. It was as if Maisie was looking at a photographic negative of herself. Maisie had curly dirty-blond hair; Hadley had curly jet-black hair. Maisie had green eyes; Hadley's were a startling light blue. Maisie's skin was golden; Hadley's was so white that the word *alabaster* from three vocabulary tests ago came to mind.

"And, in conclusion," Hadley was saying, "my great-great-grandmother was from Newport. She died young. And tragically."

As Hadley finally made her way back to her seat, Maisie saw that she had on hot-pink high tops. Maisie glanced down at her own lime-green ones and smiled. When she looked back up, Hadley was pausing by Maisie's desk, smiling right back at her.

"Harrumph!" Great-Uncle Thorne said at dinner that night when Maisie told everyone about Hadley and Rayne Ziff.

They were eating one of Maisie's least favorite dinners, *duck l'orange*, which Great-Uncle Thorne said was among the ten most civilized meals in the world. She never asked him what the other nine were because he would tell her, in excruciating detail.

"Their great-great-grandmother was from Newport," Maisie said.

"Impossible," Great-Uncle Thorne said. "I don't know anyone by the name of Ziff."

"She died young," Maisie told him. "And tragically."

"Navy brats!"

"What's wrong with the navy?" Maisie challenged as she tried to hide the greasy dark duck meat under the wild rice, which was also terrible.

"They're rapscallions, those navy kids," Great-Uncle Thorne said, motioning for Ayfe the maid to bring him more *duck l'orange*. "They have no real home, no roots. And it shows, the way they run around town without any regard for anyone or anything."

"Not all navy children—" their mother began.

But Great-Uncle Thorne boomed, "What does it matter? They come and go, like that." He snapped his fingers. "They're transient, Jennifer."

Their mother rolled her eyes.

"I'm glad there are new kids at school," she said. "It makes it more interesting."

"And they're twins," Maisie said, as if simply by having another set of twins at school meant they were destined to become friends.

"I liked being the only twins," Felix said. Their school in New York had been overflowing with twins—and two sets of triplets. But here being a twin carried a certain amount of cachet.

Felix looked at his sister, who had grown strangely still all of a sudden. He watched as a slow smile spread across her face. *What is she up to?* he wondered with a sinking feeling.

"Don't invite them to Elm Medona," Great-Uncle Thorne said, digging into his third helping of *duck l'orange*. "Who knows what they might take?"

"Take?" their mother said indignantly. "You mean steal?"

"That's right. My little Rodin I like so much, or the onyx cat from Egypt. They could slip them in their pockets and be on the next boat to Shanghai."

"Don't be ridiculous," their mother said. "I'm sure these girls are perfectly nice and not thieves at all."

As his mother and Great-Uncle Thorne talked, Felix kept his eyes on Maisie. It was almost as if he could see right into her head, as if he could see her brain working.

"I agree," Felix blurted out. "No new twins at Elm Medona."

"Felix!" his mother reprimanded.

Maisie narrowed her eyes at her brother.

"Twins," he said, meeting her gaze, "can read each other's minds. Right, Maisie?"

She didn't answer. But she didn't have to; it was a rhetorical question. She knew that Felix knew exactly what she was thinking: wouldn't it be fun to have another set of twins go into The Treasure Chest with them? Now all she had to do was figure out how to get back in there.

"Forget about it," Felix said on their way to school the next morning. "Only Pickworth twins can time travel."

"Says who?" Maisie asked.

"Great-Uncle Thorne," Felix reminded her. "That's what he told Penelope Merriweather."

They were walking down Bellevue Avenue, the broad, tree-lined street where Elm Medona sat among all of the other mansions from the Gilded Age. You couldn't see any of them; they were hidden by high walls and impressive iron gates. But signs pointed to them. *Rosecliff. Marble House. The Breakers.* Whenever he passed them, Felix wondered if those houses had rooms like The Treasure Chest, too. Or had Phinneas Pickworth been the only one with a magical room? Penelope Merriweather's father had a sarcophagus with an honest-to-goodness mummy in it right in the entry hall. But according to Penelope, almost everyone owned a sarcophagus back then. "We had such fun at parties when the sarcophagus was finally opened," she'd said dreamily.

"Are you listening to me?" Maisie demanded.

"Yes," Felix lied.

"Then what did I say?"

Felix thought for a minute.

"You said you wanted to try anyway," he said finally. "You want to bring those Ziff twins to Elm Medona, somehow get into The Treasure Chest, pick up an object, and—"

"All right, all right," Maisie muttered.

"And I say it won't work," Felix said. "First of all, there's no way to get inside—"

"There's always a way," Maisie said.

"Second of all, we'll be off who knows where, and the Ziff twins will be standing there in The Treasure Chest—"

"So what? When you brought Lily Goldberg

into The Treasure Chest, she never even knew we were gone," Maisie reminded him.

That time they'd gone all the way to China and stayed there for months. Yet, like always, when they returned it was as if no time had passed at all.

They had reached the corner of Memorial Boulevard where Jim Duncan stood waiting for them.

"If I can get in," Maisie said to Felix, "will you at least try with me?"

Felix glanced at Jim. "I don't know," he said.

"Get in where?" Jim asked.

"Nowhere," Felix answered.

Frustrated, Maisie stomped off ahead of the boys. First their father decided to get married. Then Great-Uncle Thorne decided to get married. And to throw Maisie and her family out of Elm Medona and make them move back upstairs to those dreadful servants' quarters. It was time Maisie took control of something in her life, she decided. She would figure out a way to get back inside The Treasure Chest. And then she would convince Felix to let her bring the Ziff twins there. And then—she smiled to herself—and then how could Hadley Ziff not decide that Maisie was the coolest person in the entire world? How could she not be her best friend after something like that?

Hadley Ziff walked into class late. When she did, Maisie did a double take. Hadley was wearing a white skirt with a black T-shirt, and Maisie was wearing a black skirt with a white T-shirt. Hadley noticed, too, and as she walked past Maisie's desk, she gave her a thumbs-up. For the rest of the morning, as Mrs. Witherspoon talked on and on first about pre-algebra and then about their new social studies section on inventors, all Maisie could do was watch the clock, counting the minutes until lunch, when she could finally talk to Hadley Ziff.

Sometimes time seemed to slow down when Maisie waited for something important to happen. That was how it seemed to her that morning. The two hours until lunch felt more like two *hundred* hours.

At one point, Mrs. Witherspoon said, "Maisie Robbins, do you know of any inventors to add to our list?

List? Maisie thought, looking around.

Sure enough, Mrs. Witherspoon was writing a list on the board. She stood there, a piece of chalk in one hand, staring at Maisie.

"The Wright Brothers?" Maisie said hesitantly.

Mrs. Witherspoon tapped the blackboard with her chalk hard enough to send a little puff of chalk dust into the air.

"We already *have* the Wright Brothers, Maisie," she said. "Right here beneath Thomas Edison."

Maisie saw that now that Mrs. Witherspoon had pointed it out.

"Um," Maisie said, scanning the list.

Names floated in front of her. Benjamin Franklin and Henry Ford and even Steve Jobs.

"You seem to have them all covered," Maisie said, and went back to watching the clock.

⊃

Finally, a million years later, the lunch bell rang. By then, Maisie had come up with a plan. She would be the first one at the door, and she would stand there until Hadley Ziff walked out. Then Maisie would simply fall into step beside her. They would walk together to the cafeteria, move through the food line side by side, then find a place to sit away from Bitsy Beal and her friends. By the time lunch ended twenty-three minutes later, Maisie would have invited Hadley over on Saturday. In Maisie's mind, they were already practically best friends.

Maisie was on her feet before the bell even finished ringing.

But Mrs. Witherspoon stopped her before she got to the door.

"Where is your mind today, Maisie?" she asked.

Maisie kept her eye on Hadley, who was slowly standing up and moving across the room.

"On inventors?" Maisie said.

"Please look at me when you speak to me," Mrs. Witherspoon said.

Hadley was almost at the door, and Monica Shea was making a move toward her. Monica was smart and pretty and quiet, someone Hadley might actually like.

"Mrs. Witherspoon," Maisie said as Monica reached Hadley and the two of them walked together right out the door. "I love inventors. And inventions. And I'm so excited to start this section."

She gazed up at Mrs. Witherspoon's baffled face.

"Well . . . ," Mrs. Witherspoon said.

"And also," Maisie said desperately, "I'm so hungry that I think I might faint if I don't eat something superquick."

"Well . . . ," Mrs. Witherspoon said again.

"Thanks for understanding," Maisie said, and she practically ran across the classroom and out the door.

"Go inventors!" she called over her shoulder for good measure.

Maisie stopped as soon as she left the room. The hallway had already emptied. Hadley Ziff was gone. And Monica Shea was nowhere in sight. Disappointed, Maisie began her slow, lonely walk toward the cafeteria, the same slow lonely walk she made every day. Sometimes Felix was waiting for her at a lunch table. But most times he had presidential duties to tend to—selling gross, chalky candy bars or raffle tickets, or taking a survey to measure the dissatisfaction of the sixth grade over lunch food or vending-machine goods or some other unimportant thing.

Maisie rounded the corner of the hallway that led to the cafeteria.

"There you are!" someone said, and of course

Maisie didn't look up or pause because no one was ever waiting for her.

"Maisie?" the someone said.

The someone, Maisie saw, was Hadley Ziff, who stood in front of her, grinning.

"I can't wait to hear everything you have to say about absolutely everything," Hadley said.

She crooked her arm in Maisie's.

"Go," Hadley said. "I'm all ears."

CHAPTER 3

BREAKING AND ENTERING

"Sometimes," Maisie said to Hadley Ziff, "I think my entire family is deaf. I mean, I talk and talk and talk, and either they just have blank expressions on their faces or they say *Mmmm-hmmm* in a totally fake way."

As Maisie spoke, Hadley nodded. They were standing on the corner of Bellevue Avenue and Memorial Boulevard, right where Jim Duncan had waited for Maisie and Felix just that morning. Hadley had to go right and Maisie had to go left, but neither of them wanted to part.

"Sometimes," Hadley said, "Rayne listens. But lately she's all into being popular and becoming the head of this and the head of that."

Now it was Maisie's turn to nod.

"My brother," Maisie said, lowering her voice, "is class president."

"My sister," Hadley said, also in a low voice, "was a cheerleader at our last school."

"What is wrong with them?" Maisie said sadly.

"There are times when I'm embarrassed that we share the same DNA," Hadley admitted.

They stood in a companionable silence. The trees had all sprung new green leaves and buds. On one block, a row of pink and white dogwoods had bloomed, and the petals looked pretty in the spring sunshine. Maisie remembered how much she used to like when the trees along Bleecker Street blossomed in the spring. Imagining it made her homesick.

"Do you miss San Francisco?" she asked Hadley.

"Kind of," Hadley said. "We move a lot. We've lived in Moscow and Tel Aviv and Virginia and Panama."

"I went to China once," Maisie said.

"We lived in Beijing, but just for six weeks," Hadley said.

She glanced around—nervously, Maisie thought.

"My father isn't in the navy," Hadley whispered.

"He's not?"

"He's in the CIA," Hadley said. She giggled. "I just told you my biggest secret. We're not allowed to tell people. For security reasons."

"CIA?"

"Central Intelligence Agency," Hadley explained. "It's top secret."

"What do people in the CIA do?" Maisie asked.

"Overthrow governments and all sorts of dramatic things," Hadley said. "That's why it's such a secret."

"Wow," Maisie said, impressed. She used to think having a father who was a sculptor was exciting. Until now.

Felix came down the street with a girl Maisie didn't recognize. The girl had black hair and alabaster skin, just like Hadley. But she was prettier, in the more traditional way. Her eyes were big and long-lashed. She was tall and had long legs beneath a denim skirt and blue button-down the same color as her eyes. Felix was talking, gesturing madly, and the girl couldn't take her eyes off him, as if he was the most interesting person in the world.

"Here comes Mr. President now," Maisie told Hadley, motioning her chin in Felix's direction.

"With Rayne," Hadley added.

"That's your sister?" Maisie asked rhetorically.

"Beautiful, right?" Hadley said with a sigh.

Rayne grinned when she saw Hadley and Maisie.

"Two sets of twins!" she gushed.

Felix smiled stupidly. "How about that?"

Maisie frowned at him. Hadn't he been complaining about another set of twins just last night?

"Well," Rayne said to Felix, flashing hot-pink braces on her teeth, "I'll see you Saturday."

"What's happening on Saturday?" Maisie asked Felix, who just stood there staring at Rayne Ziff like he was hypnotized.

"I'm coming to your house," Rayne said. "Felix promised to help me with my report on inventors."

Hadley looked at Maisie hopefully.

"Maybe I could come over, too?" she asked when Maisie didn't pick up her cue.

"Sure," Maisie said.

Hadley and Rayne turned to walk in the opposite direction, but Hadley paused long enough to lean close to Maisie and whisper, "I told you my biggest secret, so you have to tell me yours."

"Uh . . . okay," Maisie said, wondering if she should tell her big secret.

The Ziff twins waved good-bye, and Maisie and Felix watched them until they became just a blur.

"You invited her to Elm Medona?" Maisie blurted out. "Great-Uncle Thorne is going to be furious!"

Felix stood on tiptoe and stared down Memorial Boulevard as if he might still catch a glimpse of Rayne Ziff.

"He already kicked us out," Felix said dreamily. "What else can he do to us?"

"I don't know," Maisie said.

She tried to figure out why she felt so mad at her brother. She had wanted Hadley to come over, and now, thanks to Felix asking Rayne, Hadley would be at Elm Medona on Saturday. So she had gotten exactly what she wanted. But, Maisie reminded herself, Felix had beaten her to it. She glanced at him. *Well*, Maisie thought, *I'm not going to let him get Rayne Ziff into The Treasure Chest first. No*, she decided. On Saturday she would somehow get inside The Treasure Chest with Hadley.

Maisie broke into a grin. She did have a secret. A much better one than a father overthrowing governments. On Saturday, she would show Hadley Ziff her secret. Maisie imagined the two of them choosing an object and lifting off the ground together, tumbling through time, and landing somewhere exotic and exciting. All while Felix and Rayne wrote their reports on inventors.

"Why do you look like you're up to something?" Felix asked Maisie, sounding very much like their mother.

"Oh," Maisie said, "no reason."

"It's not going to work," Felix said as they headed down Bellevue Avenue.

"I have no idea what you're talking about," Maisie said.

"Only Pickworths can do it," Felix reminded her.

When Maisie didn't answer, he said, "Plus, The Treasure Chest is sealed up tight."

"Don't worry," Maisie said. "I'll figure something out."

Felix sighed. That was exactly what he was afraid of.

Maisie woke Saturday morning to the sound of rain falling hard. Outside, the sky was gray and stormy and the rain slapped at her windows angrily. That meant Felix's weekly Saturday baseball game would be cancelled. It meant that the four of them— Felix, Rayne, Hadley, and Maisie—would be stuck inside all day. She looked at the clock on her bedside table. She had exactly four hours to figure out how to get inside The Treasure Chest before Hadley arrived.

Someone knocked on her bedroom door.

"Come in," Maisie said, her mind already full of ideas for breaking and entering.

Her mother appeared in the doorway. "It's raining," she announced.

This was not worth answering, Maisie decided, since it was so obvious.

"A good day to spend packing up, I'm afraid," her mother said, taking in the clothes strewn around the room. She sighed. "I've grown kind of used to living in style like this."

"Me too," Maisie admitted.

"I rented another movie for us," her mother said. "*Oliver!*"

Maisie wrinkled her nose. Not one of her favorites.

"Felix and I have those new kids coming over," Maisie said.

"The twins? Don't tell Great-Uncle Thorne. He'll put everything in the safe."

Maisie laughed.

"I guess that means we'll watch the movie tonight?" her mother asked.

"Where's Bruce Fishbaum?" Maisie wondered out loud.

"His kids have school vacation this week, so he took them skiing out west," her mother said.

"Well, I'm glad we get you all to ourselves," Maisie told her.

"Even though I'm going to make you start packing?" she asked.

"Ugh."

"I'll go into town and get some boxes," her mother said.

"Don't hurry!" Maisie called after her as she left.

Maisie waited long enough for her mother to be on her way into town, then she tiptoed to the wall that hid The Treasure Chest.

Great-Uncle Thorne had sealed it so well that she couldn't even make out the edges of the door. Instead, the wall looked smooth and completely like . . . well, a wall. Maisie pushed where she thought the door was, but there was no give at all. She inched along the wall, pushing with her fingertips, hoping that she could find the spot that was actually the door that led to the staircase and The Treasure Chest. But the entire length of the wall felt solid and without any indentation.

She took a few steps back, folded her arms, and studied the wall. Maisie knew that door was there. But somehow Great-Uncle Thorne had made it seem to disappear.

"I told you," Felix said, coming to stand beside her.

"It's like it's gone," Maisie said.

They both stared at the spot where they knew the door should be. But not even the slightest crease or bump betrayed its secret location.

"Mom said I have to start packing," Felix said finally.

"Me too."

He hesitated. "She brought boxes," he said finally.

"You go ahead," Maisie said, thinking hard.

"It's useless."

"Uh-huh."

She listened as his footsteps disappeared down the hall.

Somehow she was going to get inside. She didn't know how. But Maisie was certain she would figure something out.

⌐

"You live here?" Rayne Ziff said in disbelief as she and Hadley entered the Foyer.

"Well . . . ," Felix began, but Maisie interrupted him.

"Our great-great-grandfather built it," she said. She didn't want Hadley to know yet that in one week they'd be living in the servants' quarters.

"Wow," Rayne managed.

"Come on," Felix said. "We'll show you around."

For the next hour, Maisie and Felix explained about the twenty-four–karat gold trim over here and the mantelpiece imported from the castle in France and the Flemish tapestry and the marble shipped over from Italy and the Monet painting and all the other details of Elm Medona.

"We're like the Lady in Pink," Felix said to Maisie as they stood by the dumbwaiter in the basement Kitchen.

"Where does this go?" Hadley asked, peering inside.

"Up to the servants' quarters," Maisie said.

"Can we ride in it?" Hadley asked her.

"We're not supposed to," Felix said.

Rayne had wandered up to the door that led to the railroad track that ran underground to the mansion.

"You have a train?" she asked, her eyes wide.

"Not anymore," Felix explained. "There used to be one that delivered coal here."

"So no one saw the messy stuff," Maisie added. "They hid everything unpleasant back then."

"Like what?"

"Like even delivery trucks," Maisie said. She opened the main door to show them the flower-covered arbor that hung above the driveway.

The rain still fell in a chilly, steady downpour.

They all squeezed into the doorway and looked outside.

"How many acres do you have?" Rayne asked.

"The grounds seem to go on forever."

"Can you show us around outside, too?" Hadley asked.

"Sure!" Maisie said.

"It's pouring," Rayne pointed out.

"We'll just put on our rain gear," Hadley said. "It'll be fun."

They tromped back upstairs, and everyone pulled on their rain boots and slickers.

"This is an adventure!" Hadley said, lifting the hood of her cherry-red raincoat.

Rayne tucked her pants into her leopard-patterned boots.

"Hadley loves adventures," she said with a small sigh.

"I do, too," Maisie said, sharing a smile with Hadley.

All buttoned up and booted, the four of them stepped outside into the rain.

Felix pointed out the pair of interlocking *P*s engraved on the doors and the giant peacock door knockers.

"Our great-great-grandfather built Elm Medona in 1909 as a gift to his wife, Ariane," he said.

"I hope my husband gives me a gift like this someday," Rayne said.

They made their way around the mansion, showing Rayne and Hadley the famous peonies that bloomed along one wall, the English garden with its rows of lavender and intricately carved benches, the gazebo, and the playhouse built as a miniature replica of Elm Medona.

"That's my room," Maisie said, pointing to her window. "It's named after a princess."

"And that one's mine," Felix said.

Hadley squinted. "What's that?" she said, pointing at something else.

They made their way closer to the mansion.

"Those look like naked women," Hadley said.

Maisie followed her finger straight to the Tiffany stained-glass window in The Treasure Chest.

Felix did, too. "They're goddesses," he explained. "Some famous stained-glass designer made that window for our great-great-grandfather."

"Whose room is that?" Rayne asked.

"Um," Felix said, trying to think of an answer.

"That room," Maisie said evenly, "is the best room in all of Elm Medona."

"Show us!" Hadley said with excitement.

"We can't," Felix said. "It's locked."

"Drat," Hadley said. "I want to see the best room."

A smile spread slowly across Maisie's face.

"I think you can," she said.

⊃

Felix wanted nothing to do with Maisie's scheme. But he couldn't get out of it now. That was how he found himself first dragging a ladder out of the carriage house, leaning it against the back wall of Elm Medona, and watching his sister climb all the way up to the Tiffany window.

"This is a terrible idea," Felix groaned.

But Hadley and Rayne were too excited to hear him.

"We're spies!" Rayne said. "Like Daddy!"

"*Ssshhh*," Hadley hissed at her.

From the top of the ladder, Maisie examined the window. In the rain, the colors looked gray and muted instead of bright and rich like they did when the sunlight hit them. She ran her fingers around the edges of the oval glass. And just when she was about to give up, the window budged.

"I can open it!" she called without looking down.

Hadley and Rayne cheered, but Felix only groaned again.

Maisie slid her fingers through the opening. At first, they landed on nothing but air. Then one touched the small lever that opened the window. Slowly and carefully, she turned the lever to the left, remembering her father's tip: *Righty tighty, lefty loosey*. Sure enough, the window creaked open.

"Got it!" she yelled.

She squeezed herself through the opening and landed with a soft thud smack into The Treasure Chest. Looking around at all the objects, Maisie's heart swelled. Each one offered her possibility. She picked up a magnifying glass and held it up to her eye, magnifying the objects nearby. She put that down and picked up a quill pen, then a candle, then a compass.

Behind her, someone else dropped inside. Maisie turned to see Rayne smiling at her from beneath her matching leopard rain boots and slicker.

"This is cool!" Rayne gasped. "What is all this stuff?"

Before Maisie could answer, the bottom half of Hadley appeared in the window. Her cherry-red rain boots dangled.

"Just let yourself drop down," Rayne told her.

"I'm holding the ladder while Felix climbs up," Hadley answered in a muffled voice.

Rayne and Maisie watched as Hadley finally let herself drop, followed immediately by Felix, the two of them landing in a tangled heap.

"Ouch!" Felix said.

"Welcome to The Treasure Chest," Maisie said, opening her arms wide.

"Is it a museum?" Hadley asked as she slowly got to her feet.

Maisie took a few steps toward her new friend.

"This is my secret," she whispered.

Hadley cocked her head, puzzled.

"What do you think this magnet is for?" Rayne asked, holding out a horseshoe-shaped magnet with metal reeds attached to each end.

"Put that down!" Felix said, scrambling to his feet and moving quickly toward Rayne.

Grinning mischievously, Rayne hid the magnet behind her back.

"No," she said.

"Seriously, Rayne," Felix said, "we can't touch anything in here."

"What good is having your own private . . . what did you call it, Maisie?"

"The Treasure Chest," Maisie said.

". . . your own private treasure chest if you can't play with the stuff?" Rayne continued.

Felix lunged for the magnet, but Rayne stepped away before he could reach it.

"Put it back," Felix said.

Rayne lifted the magnet close to her face. "It looks like a science experiment," she said.

"Let me see," Hadley said.

In an instant . . .

Hadley grabbed the magnet for a look.

Felix grabbed the magnet to try to get it away from Rayne.

And Maisie grabbed it because she knew, just like that, what was going to happen.

"Hey!" Rayne cried.

"What the . . . ?" Hadley said, stunned, as the four children were lifted higher and higher off the ground.

A warm wind whipped around them, carrying with it the smells of cinnamon and Christmas trees and ocean air; fresh lemons and hot chocolate and flowers in bloom.

Maisie watched Hadley's curly black hair flying as she tumbled; and Rayne's big blue eyes, wide open with surprise; and Felix's look of confusion.

They somersaulted.

Then everything stopped for the briefest instant. No smells. No sound. No motion.

And then, they dropped. Fast.

CHAPTER 4

ALEXANDER GRAHAM BELL

Felix landed with a splash.

Not a big, water-spraying splash like when he landed in the Caribbean. No, this time he landed with a small, muddy splash, smack into a puddle on a patch of soggy grass.

"Ugh!" Felix groaned, because it hurt his behind when he hit the ground and because he was now not just wet but also muddy. *Lucky I have on this rain slicker and boots*, he thought, staring up at the slate-gray sky. *Because it is raining here, too.*

In the distance, he could see a crowd of people in fancy clothes was gathered in front of a building that looked like a library: brick and imposing and serious looking.

A small voice cut through the dusk.

"What in the world . . . ?"

"Rayne?" Felix called.

"Felix?" Rayne answered, a hint of panic in her voice. "Where are we?"

Felix got to his feet and followed Rayne's voice across a small nearby knoll.

"I don't know," he admitted, helping her to her feet.

She, too, had landed in a puddle. She wiped at the mud on her jeans.

"We're not in Newport, are we?" she asked him.

Felix shook his head.

Rayne turned and watched the people milling about in front of the building ahead of them.

"Are they . . . in a play?" she asked finally.

"I would say no," Felix said. "It looks like they're going to a party or something. In there."

Now Rayne turned to face Felix, her pretty face crossed with worry.

"Why are they dressed all old-fashioned if they're not in a play?" she asked.

Felix spotted a stone bench beneath a tree.

"Come on," he said, taking Rayne's damp hand in his. "I have a lot to explain."

She let him lead her to the bench, and the two of them sat on the cold damp stone, shivering. The rain was not falling hard. Rather, it was like a relentless mist that covered everything.

"Well," Felix said, trying to figure out where to begin, "you know the room we broke into?"

Rayne nodded.

"It's full of things that my great-great-grandfather collected," Felix continued. *How*, he wondered, *do you tell someone that she has just time traveled? Or that you yourself have time traveled six other times?*

"Uh-huh," Rayne said.

"And somehow . . . I know this sounds ridiculous . . . but when Maisie and I both touch one of the objects, we . . ."

Rayne looked around again, her gaze focused on the people.

"You . . . ?" she began, but her voice broke.

"We kind of . . ."

Wonder washed across Rayne's face.

"Felix," she said, "have we *time traveled*? Are those people dressed old-fashioned because we're back when that's how everyone dressed?"

Felix watched what Rayne was watching. The men wore what almost looked like riding clothes—tight pants with tall boots and a long coat over a vest. They all had beards and held canes like Great-Uncle Thorne used. The women created a sea of blue velvet and silk long dresses and hats with feathers sticking out of them. Everyone had an umbrella, and every umbrella was black.

"Yes," Felix said, "we've time traveled."

"Where are we?" Rayne whispered, squeezing his hand—out of excitement or fear, Felix wasn't sure.

Felix stared at the people and the rain and the serious-looking people.

"I think maybe England," he guessed.

"I love England!" Rayne said, clapping her hands together. "Let's go see what the big fuss is over there, shall we?"

Felix agreed, wondering if Rayne was talking slightly British on purpose. She seemed so happy to be here that he didn't mention that they'd lost Maisie and Hadley. Or that neither of them had the magnet, and that the magnet was also the way back home. He just walked with her over to the crowd of people as if they belonged there.

Sure enough, as they got closer, everyone was speaking with a British accent. *Kind of,* Felix thought. It was British-*y*, but thicker and more garbled, harder to understand.

"They don't sound like people from England," Rayne whispered.

Before Felix could answer, a man walked out of the building and began to ring a bell, calling everyone inside.

"The show is about to begin," the man announced.

Rayne and Felix joined the crowd moving up the stairs and inside.

"Excuse me," Rayne asked the woman walking beside them. "What show is this?"

The woman cocked her head as if she couldn't quite hear her.

"Eh?" she said. "What did you say?"

"The show," Rayne said in that slow, loud way people talk when they can't be understood. "What. Is. It."

The woman smiled. "It's Professor Bell performing *David Copperfield*," she said. "You two are in for a treat. The professor reads it better than Dickens himself."

Rayne smiled at her in thanks.

The answer seemed to satisfy her, but Felix couldn't stop wondering where they were, and who they were supposed to meet.

⊃

A branch tickled Maisie's cheek. She brushed it aside and saw, across a stone stoop, Hadley sitting in a large bush, looking surprised. Maisie realized she, too, had landed in a bush. Prickly needles pressed into her legs as she tried to pull herself out. A gloved hand reached across the greenery.

"May I?" the boy attached to the hand asked.

Maisie grabbed hold, and he yanked her free.

The boy looked amused. "Didn't want to pay?" he said.

"Hey! How about me?" Hadley called.

The boy put his hands on his hips and surveyed Hadley in the bush.

"Did you think we wouldn't see you there?" he asked as he marched over to help her out.

"I have no idea what you're talking about," Hadley told him.

Across the street was a park, all soggy and gray in the drizzle. A group of boys stood there, holding a little dog by its collar.

"Haven't you come to see the talking dog?" the boy asked. He narrowed his eyes at Maisie and Hadley. "What in the world are you two wearing?"

The boy lifted the corner of Maisie's rain slicker and examined it. "I've never seen anything like this," he said. "Why, it's keeping you dry from the rain!"

"Well," Maisie said, "it's a raincoat. That's why."

He nodded. "But what is it made out of?"

"Vinyl, I think," Maisie said, realizing that vinyl had probably not yet been invented in a time when boys walked around wearing gloves and breeches and horse-drawn carriages lined the streets.

"Aleck!" one of the boys called from the park. "Hurry along now. We have to go to hear Father shortly."

The boy—Aleck—grinned at Maisie and Felix. "I won't charge you," he said. "This time."

As they followed him across the street to the park, Hadley grabbed Maisie's arm.

"Where are we?" she whispered, her voice shrill with excitement.

"The question," Maisie said, "is *when* are we."

The two girls reached the park, and Hadley took in the boys with their breeches and boots.

"Is it . . . ?" She swallowed hard. "Are we . . . ?"

Maisie nodded. "This is my secret," she said. "We've gone back in time."

Hadley's eyes shone under the lamplight.

"I always wondered if that was possible," she said. "My mother told me that my—"

"Ladies and Gentlemen," Aleck announced.

The other boys snickered.

"I shall now endeavor to have my faithful dog, Trouve, talk," he continued, ignoring them.

"He sounds British," Hadley whispered to Maisie.

"Ha!" one of the boys said, turning to her. "You're in Edinburgh, lassie. He's Scottish."

"Not after tomorrow," another boy added.

Aleck had started the dog growling, and Trouve continued without pause.

"This is talking, you say?" the tallest boy said dismissively.

At that, Aleck reached into the dog's mouth and seemed to shove his hand all the way down his throat.

"*Ow a oo ga ma*," the dog uttered.

"How are you, Grandma?" Maisie shouted. "That dog did just talk!"

"By Jove," the tall boy exclaimed. "This is much

more impressive than the automaton."

Aleck beamed at the small group before him. "After the success of that," he said, "I had to try it on a live subject."

"We built an automaton head that talked," the older boy explained to Maisie and Hadley. "I constructed the throat and larynx, and Aleck built the lips and skull."

"Melly left the hardest part for me," Aleck said.

"You see," Melly continued, "when we forced air through the windpipe with bellows, our man said *Mama*."

"That it did," the tall boy agreed. "I heard it myself."

"Just wait," Aleck said. "Some day I'll invent something that will even let Mama hear."

As if on cue, a woman holding a black umbrella over her head entered the park.

"We're going to be late," she said in slow, overly pronounced syllables.

"I'll bring Trouve upstairs," Melly said.

"Don't dillydally," their mother warned.

Aleck pressed his lips to his mother's forehead and spoke carefully. "May I bring my new friends along?"

His mother's gaze landed on Maisie and Hadley. "Peculiar clothing," she said.

"Vinyl," Aleck said, his lips moving against his mother's skin.

Maisie slipped her cold hand into her pocket, and touched the magnet there. She had a feeling that this magnet belonged to the boy standing in front her, the boy who could make a dog talk.

⊃

As soon as Felix saw Maisie and Hadley enter the theater, relief washed over him. He tried to catch his sister's attention, but she was too busy talking to the boy walking beside her. Hadley was distracted too, but not by a boy. Instead, Felix could tell by the look of wonder on her face that she was too awed by being back in time to even think about him or her sister. He saw that same look on Rayne's face as the idea of time travel settled over her.

Felix sighed, watching Maisie and Hadley, three boys, and a woman he guessed was the boys' mother make their way to the front row. He supposed there was nothing he could do now except enjoy the show.

The theater was opulent, all red velvet seats and fancy gold trim on the walls. Felix let the Scottish brogues in the air buzz in his ears. The people here were hard to understand, and for now he stopped trying and let himself sink into the plush seat.

The lights flickered.

The crowd quieted.

A lone man, distinguished looking with his thick black beard and mane of dark hair, stepped onto the stage. His piercing eyes seemed to land on every person in the audience, drawing them in. When he finally opened his mouth and spoke, his voice echoed through the theater.

Rayne pushed an elaborately printed program into Felix's hand. The man on the stage's face peered out at him, and beneath his picture, the words: PROFESSOR ALEXANDER BELL PRESENTS CHARLES DICKENS'S *DAVID COPPERFIELD*. MARCH 25, 1862. 2000 HOURS.

Hadley pointed to the date, her eyes blazing with excitement.

Felix nodded. 1862, he thought. By now he had learned enough about history to know what was happening back in the United States—the Civil War had begun, and Clara Barton was in Washington, DC, petitioning President Lincoln to let her on the battlefield. What, he wondered, was happening here in Scotland?

Professor Bell's voice, loud and authoritative, each word perfectly enunciated, interrupted Felix's thoughts. The man demanded attention, and for the next three hours, he had Felix's. And that of everyone else in that theater as well. The audience sat rapt as Professor Bell told them the story of David Copperfield, whose life in London involved enough death and love and evil characters to keep Felix on the edge of his red velvet seat.

⌐

"Stop applauding," Felix whispered to Rayne, who had jumped to her feet so enthusiastically when the curtain came down that the woman in front of them had uttered *Americans* in disgust. "We've got to get to Maisie and Hadley before they leave."

"But Felix," Rayne said, her eyes fixed on the stage where Professor Bell stood taking his bows, "that was the most amazing performance I've ever seen."

"I know," Felix said, pulling her toward the end of the row. "But if we lose them, we're in big trouble."

Luckily, the audience stayed put, applauding

through four curtain calls and allowing Felix to
practically drag Rayne to the front of the theater.

And luckily, too. Even though Hadley was as
mesmerized as her sister, Maisie was frantically
searching for Felix.

When their eyes met, Maisie broke into a smile,
waving her brother over to where she stood.

The boy next to her studied Felix and Rayne
with curiosity.

"You have these vinyl coats, too," he said.

Felix glanced down at his slicker.

"That was the most incredible show," Rayne
gushed.

"Father is said to do Dickens better than
Dickens," said the taller boy.

Maisie looked surprised. "Wait, Aleck. Professor
Bell is your father?" she asked.

The boy nodded.

In an instant, all the facts collided for Felix.

But before he could ask the question, Maisie beat
him to it.

"Then *you* must also be a Bell? Alexander—"

Aleck was nodding. "Right," he said. "Alexander
Graham Bell."

The four children looked at each other. Even if they hadn't just started a unit on inventors, they all knew the name Alexander Graham Bell.

"I know," Aleck said, misunderstanding their response. "Everyone knows Father for his work with language and sound."

Maisie laughed. "Absolutely," she said.

Melly winked at Maisie. "*Graham*," he said. "He gave himself that name to be fancy."

Aleck ignored his brother. "Are you familiar with his system of Visible Speech?" he asked eagerly.

Maisie shook her head.

"It's fascinating, really," he continued. "I'd explain more tomorrow, but I'm off to London to live with my grandfather for a year. He's quite well known himself, as a speech teacher." He lowered his voice. "I admit though, I'm a bit terrified, I am."

"You're leaving?" Felix said.

"Afraid so," Aleck said.

His family was moving toward the exit now, and a distance between the Bells and the children was developing.

Maisie stood on tiptoe. "Aleck!" she called.

But he was swept away in the crowd.

"Oh no," Felix groaned. "This is terrible."

"Why?" Hadley asked him. "We just met the person who invents the telephone. That's pretty amazing to me."

Maisie pulled the magnet out of her pocket. "We need to give this to Aleck," she explained.

"We do?" Rayne asked.

"That means we have to get to London," Felix added.

"I love London!" Rayne said happily.

"Don't you get it?" Maisie told her. "It's 1862, and we have to figure out how to get from Edinburgh, Scotland, to London."

"But first," Felix said miserably, "we need to find a place to sleep tonight."

"Maybe the Bells will let us stay with them?" Hadley said optimistically.

"I suppose we have to try that," Maisie said.

"Don't worry, Maisie," Rayne said kindly. "We'll figure it out. Meanwhile, remember what David Copperfield said? 'You'll find us rough, sir, but you'll find us ready.' That's us!"

Maisie groaned. "Great," she said. "Just great."

"Come on," Felix said, glancing around the empty

theater. "We have to get out of here and find the Bells."

"Even if they let us stay with them," Maisie said as they moved toward the exit, "we still need to find a way to get on that train to London tomorrow. If we lose Aleck, how will we ever find him in a city like London?"

"Oh!" Rayne said happily. "What an adventure!"

Maisie rolled her eyes. "You have no idea," she muttered.

They stepped out into the rainy night, the yellow glow of the gaslights hazy in the mist. The street was completely empty. No carriages. No people. It was as if the crowd and the Bells had simply vanished.

CHAPTER 5

VISIBLE SPEECH

By the time Maisie, Felix, and the Ziff twins made their way back to Charlotte Street, the light rain had turned into a steady one. They were all cold and shivering and damp, despite their rain gear. Maisie stopped in front of 13 Charlotte Street, the house she had seen Aleck's mother come out of earlier that night. Although the house was dark, Maisie climbed the stairs to the front door and gave it a tug.

Locked.

She looked down at the three worried faces on the pavement below her. Across the street, the green park where Aleck had made his dog talk appeared ominous in the darkness.

"Maybe the church is open," Hadley said,

pointing to the imposing building that took up one side of the square.

Maisie had noticed the church earlier, mostly because it didn't look like any church she had ever seen before. Large and stone, it peaked not with a steeple, but with a copper dome topped with a cross.

"That's a good idea," Felix said, bending and opening his cold toes inside his rain boots. "Churches probably stay open all night."

The four dispirited children walked to the end of Charlotte Street and turned onto George Street toward the church. It, too, was unlit, but Maisie refused to think they would not find refuge there for the night. *Felix is right*, she thought. *Churches need to stay open all night for desperate people like us.*

But the large front doors were locked tight.

"Oh no," Rayne said, close to tears.

"Don't worry," Felix told her. "We'll try the side doors, too. I just know one will be open."

They sloshed through puddles to the smaller doors on one side of the church, each lost in their own thoughts.

Felix grabbed hold of the iron handle and yanked.

The door groaned open.

Rayne let out a little yelp of happiness. The children filed in and stared upward at the vaulted ceiling. The simply decorated church stretched out in front of them. Inside felt even colder than outside.

"At least it's not raining," Felix offered, trying to stay optimistic.

One by one, they took off their dripping slickers and boots and then huddled together in a small alcove. The stone floor felt hard and cold beneath them, and they moved closer together to stay warm.

"Time traveling isn't very much fun," Rayne said sleepily.

"It'll be better tomorrow," Maisie said. "Nights can be hard. But you'll see. We'll find Aleck and go to London and have a wonderful adventure."

"How can you be sure?" Hadley asked.

Felix sighed. "That's just how it works," he said.

And then, despite everything, he fell right to sleep.

Felix woke to the sound of footsteps echoing across the stone floor and keys rattling noisily. He opened his eyes just as an old man stopped at the pile of children.

"What have we here?" the man said, his accent even harder to understand than everyone else Felix had heard so far.

Hadley rubbed at her eyes and looked around, confused.

"Wha—?" she began, jumping to her feet. Then, as if she remembered, she nodded to herself and slowly sunk back down.

"I'm sorry, sir," Maisie piped up. "Our door was locked, and it was raining and—"

The man furrowed his stiff silver eyebrows.

"I can't understand a word you're saying," he said. "You must be some of the deaf children Professor Bell teaches?"

Felix and Maisie looked at each other, both of them smiling slightly.

Maisie nodded. "We are," she said.

"Well, let's go then," the man said, already turning to leave. "I'll show you which house is his. It's number thirteen. Thirteen Charlotte Street, right around the corner."

Rayne slept through this entire interaction. Hadley had to nudge her awake and help her get back into her rain boots and slicker so that they could keep up with the old man and Maisie and Felix, who were hurrying through the church to the big front doors.

They stepped outside into the same steady rain that had made them so miserable the night before.

"Does it *always* rain here?" Maisie said grumpily.

The man chuckled. "It is Scotland, after all, isn't it?"

The trees in Charlotte Square seemed silver in the early morning light as the children walked down George Street. In the distance, green hills rose and a river cut through them.

The man saw Maisie admiring the view.

"Them's the Fife Hills, and that's the Firth of Forth," he said. He pointed in the other direction. "And them's the Pentland Hills."

He took a moment to also admire the view.

"Scotland," he said, with a smile and a nod.

At the Bell's house, the man banged the knocker twice and waited.

Soon enough, Melly Bell, Aleck's brother, opened the door.

"I've got the professor's students here," the man told him.

Melly frowned in confusion.

"Thank you, Mr. MacGregor," he said, opening the door wider to let the four children in.

The foyer into which they entered was square and dimly lit by a gas lamp that cast a warm yellow glow. In front of them, a staircase wound upward, and Melly pointed toward it, indicating they should go upstairs.

At the landing, Maisie, who led the way, paused.

"One more," Melly told her.

She climbed the winding staircase to the next floor, waiting for the others there. A large chandelier hung above the narrow hall, where two doors sat shut. The smell of gas hung in the air.

Melly reached the landing and went to open the door for them. With his hand on the knob, he turned to Maisie.

"Weren't you the lot at the performance last night?" he asked her.

Maisie nodded.

"Did you forget to tell Father that you were here for a lesson?"

Maisie hesitated, then nodded again.

Melly seemed to accept this, as he opened the door and let them inside, calling to his father as he did.

Professor Bell and Aleck came into the front sitting room, both of them looking harried.

"They're here for lessons," Melly explained.

"Now?" Professor Bell said. "But we have to get Aleck off to the train in a few hours."

Without waiting for anyone to reply, Professor Bell said, "Very well," as if he'd made up his mind right then. "Hang up their coats, Melly, and tell your mother to send out some tea. And biscuits?" he added, directing this question to the children.

"Yes, please," Rayne said through a yawn.

"Aleck, maybe you can help me out here," Professor Bell said.

"I'm happy to take a break from packing my trunk," Aleck admitted.

Professor Bell retrieved a large poster from one corner of the room. He took some time placing it on an easel and adjusting it so that everyone could see. As he set this up, Mrs. Bell came into the room with a tray. On it was a large teapot, six cups, and a tray of sweets as well as a pitcher of cream. She set it on the table, then poured cream into each cup before filling them with tea.

"Please," she told the children, who eagerly

reached for the sweets first.

As soon as she left the room, Professor Bell faced the children, their mouths full of cake.

"Visible Speech," he said, tapping the poster. "Here are the thirty-four symbols that show every sound a human mouth can make."

At the top of the poster was a line drawing of a face, with an arrow pointing out of the mouth.

The bottom was a confusing array of charts and figures. Felix tried to make sense of it, but he couldn't.

"In a moment," Professor Bell said, "Aleck and I will do a little demonstration. But first, Aleck, would you recite something to show the children here what good elocution sounds like? Watch his lips and tongue as he speaks," he directed.

Aleck stepped forward. He cleared his throat and lifted his chin, throwing his shoulders back.

"How doth the little busy bee," he began, "improve each shining hour? And gather honey all the day, from every opening flower."

"His lips definitely looked different for different letters," Maisie said.

Professor Bell nodded enthusiastically. "Exactly! That is why I believe my system can teach the deaf to speak. And if they can learn to speak, they'll be allowed to go to school and to get jobs."

"Shall I?" Aleck asked.

His face showed how proud he was of his father's system. Felix thought of his own father, how proud he'd feel when he and Maisie would come to his studio and he could show them his latest paintings.

Aleck left the room, and Professor Bell took the poster off the easel and rested it on a table so that they could still see it. He replaced it on the easel with a large pad of paper.

"Give me some words," he asked them.

"Rain," Hadley said.

"Cake," Rayne said, taking the last piece from the plate.

"Good!" Professor Bell said, busily writing symbols on the paper. "Another?"

"Home," Felix said.

The professor called for Aleck to return.

"Here I've written your words in my Visible Speech symbols. Aleck, can you read the words?"

Aleck looked at what his father had written. To Maisie, the symbols looked a little like Greek letters and a little like the iron from her Monopoly game.

But Aleck quickly said, "Rain. Cake. Home." He added, "Easy ones."

Professor Bell beamed. "With this system, we can change the lives of the deaf."

"And with science," Aleck added. "Even if I run off to sea someday—"

His father interrupted. "Hogwash!"

"I'll still figure out a way to use sound to help the deaf hear," he said, ignoring his father.

Maisie and Felix glanced at each other.

"I believe you will," Maisie said quietly.

"But for now, you are off to London, son," Professor Bell said.

He handed the children a sheaf of paper.

"Practice these elocution lessons. The busy-bee one is there. Start with that. And we'll continue next week," he told them.

"Um . . ." Maisie stammered. "Um . . ."

Professor Bell shook his head. "Please," he said, as if she'd hurt his ears. "Never utter that again."

"It's just that we can't come next week because . . . um . . ."

He glared at Maisie and she clapped her hand over her mouth.

"Because *we're* going to London, too!" Felix blurted.

"What a strange coincidence," Professor Bell said. "Shall we take you in our carriage to the station?"

"That would be lovely," Hadley chimed in.

"And your parents are meeting you there?" Professor Bell asked.

"That's another coincidence," Maisie said. "We were here visiting *our* grandfather, and now we're going *home* to London."

Professor Bell looked skeptical.

The four children held their breath until he said, "We are departing promptly at noon."

Rayne glanced out the large window covered with rain, then back at the Professor.

"You're free to wait here," he said.

Aleck and his father started to leave the room.

"Excuse me," Rayne said. "Is there any more cake?"

"I'll see what I can find," the professor said with a scowl.

Rayne rewarded him with her brightest smile, which made Professor Bell smile, too.

Maisie watched this with a combination of annoyance and awe. Rayne Ziff was one of those girls who could bat her eyelashes and show off her dimples and get anything she wanted. Including, Maisie thought, her brother, Felix, who was watching her with puppy-dog eyes. But as annoying as that kind of girl could be, when you are homeless and hungry on a rainy day in Scotland, staying warm by a fire and eating cake was not a bad thing.

Rayne, Maisie decided, was coming in very handy.

CHAPTER 6

NUMBER 18 HARRINGTON SQUARE

At the train station, the children busied themselves with staring up at the ornate vaulted ceiling and gaping at the people waiting for trains.

"Everyone is so fancy," Rayne said, admiring the hat of a woman standing beside them. It was dark brown velvet with a large peacock feather hanging from it.

"Every*thing* is so fancy," Hadley added.

The Bell family stood just a short distance away from them. Felix and Maisie watched Professor and Mrs. Bell saying good-bye to Aleck, who looked miserable over leaving home.

"How do you propose we pay for tickets on that train to London?" Felix whispered to his sister.

"I'm figuring that out right now," she said.

"Sure," Felix said, feeling as miserable as Aleck looked.

Actually, Maisie did have a plan. She was just waiting for the right time to implement it.

And the right time presented itself at that very moment.

The big board with the list of train arrivals and departures that hung from the ceiling of the station went into action. Letters and numbers flipped and rotated upward and there at the top was the train to London. In the distance, Maisie could hear it rumbling down the tracks. It let out a long, low whistle.

As soon as the whistle died out, Maisie shouted, "Our tickets! Our tickets! Someone has stolen our tickets!"

She patted her pockets frantically.

It seemed that every person in the train station turned to look at Maisie.

"Poor child," the woman with the fancy hat said.

"It's the pickpockets," added a man who looked very much like a penguin, shaking his head.

"How will we ever get to London to see our parents?" Maisie cried.

Felix stared at her with a mixture of embarrassment and admiration.

Out of the corner of her eye, Maisie saw Mrs. Bell whispering to her husband, a worried look on her face.

"And with Mother sick, this will just ruin her," Maisie added.

For effect, she covered her face in her hands until she heard footsteps approaching. She let herself smile a little before she dropped her hands and gazed up into Professor Bell's face.

"Now, now," he said, "don't be upset. We'll get you new tickets."

"You will?" Felix blurted.

"Oh, we couldn't," Maisie said. "You've already been so kind."

"The pickpocket problem is a travesty," Professor Bell said. "And to steal from children . . . well, it's just unconscionable."

The train appeared, chugging to a stop in front of them.

"Wait right here," Professor Bell said, and off he went to the ticket window.

By the time the passengers had unloaded and

new passengers had lined up to board, Maisie was holding four tickets to London in her hand.

⊃

Aleck sat beside Felix on the train, but he didn't speak much. Instead, he stared out the window, gazing at the passing landscape blurred by rain.

"Where does your grandfather live?" Felix asked him.

Too often he and Maisie had lost track of the person they met and then they spent too much time trying to find that person again. This time he wanted an address.

"On Harrington Square," he said without looking at Felix. "Right across from Harrington Gardens."

"Harrington Square," Felix repeated the address help himself memorize it. "Across from Harrington Gardens."

Now Aleck did turn to face Felix. "Do you know it?" he asked.

"Um. Yes?" Felix said hesitantly. What if Aleck asked him questions about it? But this way when Aleck saw them nearby, he wouldn't think it strange.

Aleck gave a little nod and turned his attention back to staring out the window.

Behind them, the girls whispered together.

"How do you do it?" Hadley was asking Maisie.

"I don't know *why* it works," Maisie said. "All I know is that we both, or should I say *all*, have to hold an object. We have to have the shard with us—"

"What shard?" Rayne asked.

Maisie pulled the shard from the Ming vase from her pocket.

"This," she said. "For some reason we can't time travel without it, so I always keep it on hand."

Rayne and Hadley studied the shard in Maisie's upturned palm.

"And," Maisie added, closing her fingers around the shard and tucking it back in her pocket, "it only works with twins."

"How do we get back?" Hadley asked, her voice suddenly serious.

"We give the object to Aleck," Maisie said.

She hesitated.

"And, this is tricky, but he has to give us advice or information or something. That's the hard part," she said, thinking about Great-Aunt Maisie.

"Have you given him the magnet?" Rayne asked her.

Maisie shook her head. "Not yet."

Hadley's face was scrunched with concentration. "We'd better stay close to Aleck," she said finally. "If we lose him, we won't get back. Right?"

"That's right," Maisie said. She grinned at Hadley. "So," she said, "how do you like my secret?"

Hadley grinned, too. "It's a good one."

Maisie settled back in her seat, feeling happy.

"And Felix said only Pickworths could do it," she said, more to herself than to the other girls.

"What did you say?" Hadley asked her.

"Oh, nothing," Maisie said. "Felix tried to convince me that it wouldn't work with you and Rayne."

"But you said something about Pickworths, didn't you?" Hadley said.

"That's my great-great-grandfather, who built Elm Medona and put all the stuff in The Treasure Chest," Maisie explained. "Phinneas Pickworth."

Hadley and Rayne looked at each other. Then they looked at Maisie, both of their face awash in surprise.

"What?" Maisie said.

"Our great-great-grandmother was *Amy* Pickworth," Rayne gushed. "Phinneas Pickworth's twin sister."

Felix's head popped over the seat in front of them. Although they had been whispering about The Treasure Chest, this news was given loudly.

"Amy Pickworth?" Felix said. "But she disappeared in the Congo when she was sixteen."

Rayne was nodding. "Remember I said we had a relative from Newport who died tragically? That was Amy Pickworth."

Maisie tried to take in this information, but it didn't quite make sense.

"But if she's your great-great-grandmother, she had a baby when she disappeared?"

"Right," Hadley said. "They got married young in those days. She married some duke who was killed in a battle. He never even met his daughter."

"He died before she was born," Rayne added. "Amy and her brother Phinneas left her baby with the nursemaid like they used to do in those days and went to the Congo for big-game hunting to lift her spirits."

"And she disappeared," Hadley finished.

"But," Maisie said happily, "this makes us related!" The four children all smiled at each other.

⊃

When the train pulled into the station in

London, the four children stayed close by Aleck. This made Felix feel better, not just because they needed to stick with him, but also because the station was enormous and crowded. People jostled past them and crushed against them as they moved toward the main doors.

"You won't be able to miss my grandfather," Aleck said. "He wears a big gray beaver hat. You've never seen anything like it," he added with a chuckle. "It was in style when he was a young man, and he's never been able to part with it."

"That must be him then," Maisie said, pointing.

"Indeed!" Aleck said.

The old man looked very much like Aleck, Felix thought, with his piercing black eyes and a rather large hooked nose. His hair was white, but he had a lot of it, and his face looked kind.

"I'd recognize that Bell nose anywhere, my boy," Grandfather Bell said, taking Aleck into a bear hug.

When he released Aleck, Aleck turned to the others.

"It's been nice meeting you all," he said.

"Aren't you going to Harrington Square?" Felix said quickly before the Bells could walk away.

"Yes," Grandfather Bell answered.

"So are we!" Felix said.

"Is your mother meeting you here?" Aleck asked him.

"She's sick," Maisie interjected. "Remember?"

"Come on then," Grandfather Bell said. "We'll drop you."

Relieved, they followed him out into the early London evening.

To Maisie's horror, the air stunk like nothing she'd ever smelled, and her stomach immediately started to churn.

"What is that smell?" she asked from behind the hand she'd placed over her nose and mouth.

"I think it's every horrible smell there is," Hadley said, her nose wrinkled in disgust.

"You've been in Scotland so long you've forgotten the beautiful aromas of London, have you?" Grandfather Bell said with a big belly laugh. "That's horse manure and the sewage in the Thames and all sorts of other unpleasant things."

It does smell bad, Felix thought. But he was more taken aback by how it looked. Even though it was not yet six o'clock, the city was dark with black smoke and thick with a yellow fog that seemed to go on for miles. The combination seemed to wrap around him and fill his lungs. He coughed. And then his eyes started to water.

"Take each other's hands now," Grandfather Bell ordered, "so you don't get lost in the fog."

"Does that actually happen?" Felix asked in a trembling, choked voice.

Rayne took his hand and squeezed gently.

"Just yesterday a man drowned in the Thames when he fell in because he couldn't see it," Grandfather Bell said.

The street was more crowded than even Times Square in New York City. And muddier than anything any of them had ever seen before.

But what caught Maisie's attention was how many children clogged the street. Dressed in ragged clothes, some of them even barefoot, all of them with dirt-streaked legs and cheeks, the children seemed to be in perpetual motion. They ran to open cab doors. They held on to horses' reins. They carried brightly wrapped packages for women in fine clothes. They yelled at passersby to buy oranges or matches or flowers from them.

A boy stopped right in front of them, looked at Grandfather Bell, and broke into a series of cartwheels, right through the mud.

"Ha' penny, sir?" he asked hopefully when he was upright again.

Grandfather Bell tossed the boy a coin.

"Orphans," he said, shaking his head sadly. "So many orphans."

Maisie thought of the movie *Oliver!* that her mother liked to watch so much. It had been a play, too, and her mother had been in during that long-ago summer when she'd met Maisie's father. They were going to watch it that very night. Now she wished she had paid closer attention. The movie was about London right around this time, and orphan children who become pickpockets to survive. She turned to whisper this to Felix, but Grandfather Bell had hailed a cab and everyone was already piling in. Maisie picked her way through the muddy street and followed them.

The city was so noisy that even inside the cab the sounds of dozens of horses' hooves beating on the pavement, wheels clacking, bells ringing, peddlers calling out, music playing—some kind of brass band, a clarinet, and the tinny grind of an organ—could all be heard.

"There's so much I want to show you, boy," Grandfather Bell told Aleck as they moved through the crowded streets. He spoke loudly to be heard over the cacophony that penetrated the cab. "But I'm afraid it will have to wait until morning. I have a class tonight."

"That's all right," Aleck said. "I'd love to sit in on your class, if you'll let me." He looked at the children and added, "Grandfather Bell is an elocutionist."

"An *elo-what*?" Rayne asked.

"He teaches people to speak correctly," Felix told her.

"I'd love to come, too," Maisie said suddenly.

"Well, I—" Grandfather Bell began, but Maisie interrupted him.

"We took a class with Aleck's father just this morning. Lips and tongues and everything," she said.

"It's rather unorthodox—"

"Do you say things like '*The rain in Spain falls mainly on the plain*'?" Rayne asked.

"Well—"

"Oh! I do hope you do that exercise," she said, turning her pretty blue eyes on the old man hopefully.

"All right then," Grandfather Bell said with a deep sigh. "But you must all be very quiet so the girls don't feel self-conscious."

The cab came to a stop then, and out of nowhere a young boy, no more than six or seven years old, appeared from the shadows and opened the door for them.

Another one just a bit older swept the street in front of them as they walked.

"Orphans," Grandfather Bell said again softly as he tossed half pennies at the boys.

Maisie watched as the two little boys ran off to meet another cab approaching the square. At least she and the others had a warm house to go into, and parents back home, and food and water and beds and . . . *Oh!* she thought. *Stop counting your blessings.* After all, she didn't know what was going to happen to them next here in 1862.

CHAPTER 7

ENTERING THE PARISH

Grandfather Bell settled them all in the drawing room, which looked like a living room to Maisie with its arrangement of sofas and chairs. A coal fire burned in the fireplace, and the children sat close to it for warmth. Outside, darkness had fallen and even with the streetlamps lit, Maisie couldn't see the gardens across the street.

A maid in a gray uniform with a white apron and cap came in wheeling a small cart of sandwiches and tea. Maisie watched Felix survey the sandwiches suspiciously. She was hungry enough to eat almost anything, but Felix could be persnickety. Apparently, he was the only fussy one, though. Hadley and Rayne looked ready to dig in.

Aleck helped himself right away, filling a plate with sandwiches and little triangular scones. He spooned some jam onto the side of his dish, and then added what looked like spoiled cream.

Maisie did exactly as he did, but paused over the cream.

"Is this okay to eat?" she asked him.

"I would think so," Aleck said, amused. "It's clotted cream."

Hadley and Rayne took some of everything, but Felix wrinkled his nose at the word *clotted*. He decided to stick with just jam. One type of sandwich appeared to be cucumbers with butter, a favorite of Great-Aunt Maisie. Another had some dry gray meat in it and bright green jelly. Felix passed on those. He decided that if he had to paint the city of London, he would use the color gray for almost everything.

By the time they'd finished eating, Grandfather Bell's students had started to arrive. About ten women made their way into the drawing room, removing hats and gloves and finding seats, chattering together as they did.

"They all look so pretty!" Rayne said with a sigh.

"Can you Adam and Eve it?" one of them said, peering at the five children. "I was going up the apples and pears and thought I 'eard dustbin lids up 'ere."

"Dustbin lids?" Hadley repeated.

Even Aleck looked confused at what she said.

The woman laughed. *She's young, like Miss Landers,* Felix thought. Up close like this, he could see that the fabric of her dress was worn in spots and slightly frayed at the hem. Her hands were rough and red, and some of her teeth were gray. Yet somehow she was pretty despite that.

"I've been on my plates all day," she said as she dropped onto one of the chintz-covered chairs.

She pointed a finger at Felix.

"Use your loaf, boy!" she said. "I'm a working girl."

That made all the other women laugh, too.

Grandfather Bell's voice broke through the laughter.

"That slaughtering of the English language," he said in his precisely enunciated words, "is what is called Cockney."

"Like Eliza Doolittle," Maisie whispered to Felix.

Felix thought of the young and pretty Audrey

Hepburn and tried to imagine *this* woman singing "Wouldn't It Be Loverly?"

"It's like we've stepped right into a scene from *My Fair Lady*," Rayne said softly.

"Translation," Grandfather Bell said. "'Apples and pears' is stairs. 'On her plates' means on her feet. And 'use your loaf—'"

"Means use your loaf!" the woman interrupted cheerfully.

Grandfather Bell shook his head. "This one," he said, "is impossible. I would like to take her for six months and teach her to speak not just better English, but the King's English. Then I would buy her a beautiful gown and take her to the fanciest ball in London. I'd dare anyone to discover that she was really a Cockney peddler and not a society woman."

"But that's what Henry Higgins does!" Felix blurted.

"'enry 'iggins?" the woman said. "Who's 'e?"

"I have no earthly idea," Grandfather said.

He opened a heavy book with gold-trimmed pages. THE COLLECTED WORKS OF WILLIAM SHAKESPEARE was written across the cover in dark red script.

"Shall we?" he asked—rhetorically, Maisie thought.

"Enough wit' this rabbit and pork," the woman said, rubbing her hands over the fire. "On to *'amlet*!"

For two hours the women took turns reading parts of *Hamlet* out loud. They weren't all Cockney. Some had different kinds of accents; some seemed just to be shy. To those, Grandfather Bell ordered, "Project! Project your voice! Throw it to the farthest wall!"

"Until next week," he said when the clock struck eight.

The women gathered their things, pinning their hats and pulling on gloves.

"And," Grandfather Bell added, looking at the children, "good night to all of you as well."

Aleck yawned. "It's been a big day," he said.

Maisie fingered the magnet in her pocket, its metal cold against her hand. Was this the time to give it to Aleck? Or should she wait?

"Normally we would have supper now," Grandfather Bell said. He patted Aleck on the shoulder. "But you should turn in early tonight."

Maisie pulled the magnet from her pocket.

"Aleck," she said, feeling Felix and Hadley and

Rayne watching her, "I wanted to give you this. For your experiments with sound."

"A magnet?" Aleck asked her.

He took it from her and examined the various reeds attached to either end.

"What are these for?" he wondered out loud.

"You'll figure it out," Maisie said.

"Well," Aleck said, placing the magnet on the table, "thank you."

Maisie realized that the maid had appeared with all of their raincoats.

"Nancy will show you out," Grandfather Bell said.

What could they do except slip into their slickers, go out to the hall where their boots waited for them, and then go outside into the dark, rainy, smelly London night?.

"What if we don't see the Thames and we fall in and drown?" Felix asked as they stood on the street trying to decide where to go.

Felix pronounced it *Tames*, which was how *Thames Street* in Newport was pronounced.

"It's *Thames*," Hadley said, emphasizing the *th* sound.

"I don't care what you call it," Felix groaned. "I don't want to drown in it."

Maisie peered around the corner. The main streets were lit by gas lamps. In fact, when they'd arrived at Grandfather Bell's house, a man was going around lighting the lamps with a big pole that had a fixture on one end. She'd watched as he inserted it into each lamppost and a sudden burst of flame ignited inside.

"You look like you've never seen a lamplighter," Grandfather Bell had teased her.

Now she wished there had been more lamplighters around. The side streets had no lights at all. They yawned out into sheer darkness as a swirl of fog floated eerily around everything.

"I don't think we should leave the main street," Maisie decided.

"We can't just stand here all night," Rayne said.

They agreed on that, but none of them had any idea what to do. Felix's bringing up the man who drowned in the Thames because he couldn't see it had frightened them. Now they didn't want to wander too far off. The dark, foggy streets added to their growing fear.

From the distance, the sound of heavy footsteps moved toward them.

"Oh dear," Rayne whispered as they inched closer together.

Out of the darkness stepped a man. He wore a long, dark coat with big brass buttons and a thick belt around his waist. They all noticed his shiny top hat. But only Maisie noticed his gun.

"Where do you belong?" the man barked at them.

Maisie's eyes drifted from that gun hanging from his belt up to the badge pinned to his coat. She could just make out the words CITY POLICE with a crown etched above them.

Just as she felt relieved that this wasn't a bad guy, the policeman grabbed Felix roughly by the ear and yanked him closer.

"Come on, then," he said in disgust. "The lot of you."

For a brief moment Maisie considered running away. But how would she ever find her brother again if she left him now? At least the police would bring them somewhere warm for the night, maybe even give them some food.

"Thank you, Officer," Maisie said as she fell into step beside him.

The policeman laughed.

"You're thanking me for bringing you to the workhouse?" he scoffed. "That's a good one."

"Workhouse?" Maisie repeated.

But the policeman didn't answer her. He didn't let go of Felix either.

Maisie turned to see what Hadley and Rayne thought of this situation. But when she did, they were gone. All she saw was an empty street and the fog swirling around the lampposts.

To Felix, the workhouse looked like a prison.

Once the policeman deposited them there, a fat woman with red cheeks and watery eyes handed the twins scratchy, tattered uniforms and ordered them to put it on. Then she half-dragged, half-led Maisie to a set of big double doors and told her to find an empty cot and get some sleep. She grabbed Felix by the ear the policeman had left alone and brought him to another set of double doors, instructing him to do the same.

"You'll need your sleep," she said in an accent like some of the women in Grandfather Bell's class had. "Sweepin's hard work."

"Sweeping?" Felix repeated.

But the woman just folded her arms and glared at him.

Reluctantly, Felix walked through those doors into a big room. As far as he could see, cots stood in rows. On each cot, there was a small lump of a boy.

Felix walked slowly up and down each row, looking for an empty one.

"*Pssst,*" he heard. "Over 'ere."

Felix followed the voice several rows over.

"Take Jimbo's," the boy said. "'e won't be needin' it anymore."

Felix crawled under the thin blanket.

"Where did . . . um . . . Jimbo go?" he asked the boy.

"Dead," the boy said matter-of-factly.

Felix shivered under the dead boy's blanket.

"What happened to him?" he managed to ask.

The boy snorted. "'e died!"

"I . . . I know. But how?"

"'ow would I know? 'e got sick and 'e died. Maybe quinsy. 'e complained about his throat."

"But—" Felix began.

"They take the dead ones and put them in meat

pies," the boy whispered. "And that's the truth."

"I don't think—"

"You're in the parish now," the boy said sleepily. "You'll get used to it."

The boy settled back onto his own cot.

All around him, Felix heard the soft breathing and light snores of sleeping children.

Orphans! Grandfather Bell had said.

And now Felix was one of them.

⌐

Felix was awakened from a fitful sleep by someone hitting the bottoms of his feet with a stick.

"Get up, you little buggers," a man growled.

Through his half-opened eyes, Felix watched the man move systematically up and down the rows of cots, slapping all the boys awake the same way.

No one hesitated. As soon as the stick left a boy's feet, the boy jumped up, cowlicks pointing to the ceiling, eyes filled with sleep. Felix did the same, the bottoms of his feet still smarting and both of his ears hot and sore from the night before.

The boy in the cot next to him grinned down at Felix. He was tall and stout, with black soot in his sandy hair and around his ears and neck.

"You can be my climbing boy, Jimbo the Second," he said.

The sound of the dead boy's name sent a shudder down Felix's spine.

"Felix," he said quickly. "My name is Felix."

"Stop the yammering!" the man yelled. "Get to breakfast so you can get to work!"

The boys formed a ragtag line and slowly made their way out.

"Breakfast," the boy muttered. "Gruel is all we get. Call it what you like."

They moved down the corridor to another vast room, this one with rows and rows of long tables and chairs. Already half the room was filled with girls, and Felix searched for any sign of Maisie among them.

"Looking for someone?" the boy asked him.

"My sister," Felix said.

"So you just got put out then?" the boy asked.

Felix took a seat next to him but kept his eyes searching the rows of girls.

"You still remember your mum? And eating bangers and mash?" the boy continued.

Hot tears sprung to Felix's eyes. He didn't know what bangers and mash was, but surely it was better than gruel. And the thought of his mother made his chest ache with homesickness.

"I 'ardly remember mine," the boy said softly. "She smelled nice, I think. She sang to me at night."

Felix looked at the boy, but the boy looked away.

"No use complainin', is there?" he said.

A woman even fatter than the one last night moved through the rows with a big pot. She reached Felix's table and ladled what looked like thin oatmeal into his bowl. One ladle full barely covered the bottom. But that was all each boy got before she moved on to the next one.

"Get used to it," the boy said, spooning some into his mouth. "It's breakfast. It's lunch. And it's dinner."

Another boy was so thin and sallow-complexioned that Felix wondered if he had quinsy, too, whatever that was. His large brown eyes were sunk deep into his head and when he smiled he showed a mouth of rotten teeth.

"Don't lie to the new boy, Johnny," the sallow boy said. "Sometimes we get meat or potatoes thrown in."

"Practically never," Johnny said.

"Sweeps!" someone bellowed, and boys rushed to their feet.

Johnny tugged on Felix's collar.

"That's us," he said, pulling him from his seat.

Felix followed Johnny to the door where boys were lining up. He craned his neck, still searching the girls' side of the cafeteria for Maisie. Just when he thought he glimpsed her tangle of blond hair, the boys began to move out. He stood on tiptoe and waved his hand in her direction.

But as soon as he did, a stick came out of nowhere. *Smack!* Right down on his shoulder.

"Move it, sweep," one of the guards bellowed at him.

And in an instant, Felix was out in the rainy, foggy, stinking London air again.

CHAPTER 8

CHIMNEY SWEEPS AND ORANGE SELLERS

Sweeps.

Felix mulled over the word as he and a few dozen other boys left the workhouse—the *parish*—and stood in the still-dark early-morning light. The smell of manure and sewage and smoke filled the air.

Sweeps.

He finally supposed that he would be handed a broom and taken to some dirty house or building and made to sweep up. *Like a janitor*, Felix decided. *That isn't too bad*, he told himself. He'd swept up at home before. Why, he had experience as a sweep!

Felix didn't notice the skinny, bent man in the dirty coat arrive.

But Johnny did. He nudged Felix in the ribs and whispered, "'ere we go now, mate."

The man spit an address at Johnny, but Felix didn't understand him.

Johnny let out a low whistle.

"May Fair," Johnny said, picking up a broom from a wheelbarrow the man had parked on the street corner. "Posh."

The man asked Johnny a question. Again Felix didn't understand him.

"My new climbing boy," Johnny told him, slapping Felix on the back.

As they walked off, Felix imagined that as the climbing boy he'd have to clean the second floor of these . . . what had Johnny called them? *Posh*. Posh apartments. That was all right. He held tight to the broom he'd taken from the wheelbarrow.

"You're not afraid of small places?" Johnny asked at one point.

Felix thought of the dumbwaiter back in Elm Medona.

"Well, I don't like them much," he said. "Especially if it's dark inside."

"*Hmmm*," Johnny said.

They kept walking, Johnny whistling softly as they did.

"Where is this May Fair?" Felix asked after some time. His eyes had started to tear from the smoke and soot in the air.

"Almost there," Johnny said.

But they weren't. They just kept walking through streets much like the one near the train station the day before.

Had that only been the day before? Felix thought sadly. A warm fire. Tea and sandwiches. His stomach grumbled. The gruel this morning had been thin and meager. He wished he had some of that gray meat with green jelly now. The relentless noise of the city pounded in Felix's head. *It would actually be nice to get into someone's posh house and sweep up their dusty floors*, he thought.

Finally Johnny came to an abrupt halt.

"It's this row," he said, pointing to a block of identical row houses.

"All of them?" Felix said. The houses were tall and skinny. He counted eight on the block.

"'fraid so," Johnny said cheerfully.

Each house had a wrought iron gate in front of

steep steps leading to the front doors, double-glass affairs with lace curtains hanging on them. There were lace curtains in all the windows, too, and behind some of them a warm, soft light glowed. That light made Felix even sadder. Inside were families, families waking up and eating toast and laughing together. Families unaware of how precious mornings were in their quiet, cozy houses.

He moved to open the gate of the first house, just to get started, to push away his sadness.

But Johnny clasped his big hand over Felix's.

"We go up through the cellar, mate," he said. "They don't want the likes of us traipsing through their drawing rooms and parlors, do they?"

He didn't wait for an answer. Instead he tugged Felix away from the gate and down an alley stinking of trash and rotting things. Felix saw a long, skinny tail disappear in the garbage and forced himself to look up, straight ahead.

Behind the house was a small, neat yard with a little garden. Johnny and Felix walked through it to the cellar bulkhead. There Johnny paused.

"It's a little scary the first time," he said. "I started as a climbing boy, before I had me growth spurt and got so big. And Mr. Pippin? The bloke who gave us our assignment this morning? 'e was me boss." He lowered his voice. "'e lit *fires* beneath me to get me moving, 'e did. I still got scars on the soles of me feet from the blisters. And me only six years old at the time. Me mum just dead. Me 'eart broken."

"Fires?" Felix said, confused.

Johnny nodded. "I vowed that if I lived, and if I ever got me a climbing boy, I wouldn't do *that*, no sir."

"Okay," Felix said slowly. He was missing something, of that he was certain. But what?

"It's not too bad," Amelia said to Maisie.

They were in a place called Convent Garden, an enormous place that sold every kind of food imaginable. Amelia and Maisie were there to get oranges. "We'll sell them in the West End," Amelia had told Maisie after breakfast. "We'll make a few pence. You'll see."

But first they had to come here and buy the oranges.

"Just got to get past the costermongers," Amelia said, weaving her way through hundreds of men buying fish to sell.

Maisie put her hand over her nose and mouth again and concentrated on staying close to Amelia, whose red hair made her easy to follow. She had freckles, too—more than Maisie had seen on any one person. Small and skinny with creases of dirt in her neck, Amelia couldn't be more than eight or nine years old. But when Maisie had asked her how old she was, the girl had just looked surprised. "Well, I have no idea!" she'd said brightly.

At breakfast, as Maisie sat sullenly eating the disgusting oatmeal they'd slopped into her bowl, Amelia had offered to take her with her to sell oranges on the street. "Better than breaking rocks," Amelia had added. That was when Maisie thought she saw Felix. Or at least the top of what looked like his head. *Maybe it had been a mirage*, she thought now as the sight of a stall of oranges finally came into view. It had been just a flash of hair that looked like his. Maybe she'd even seen the outline of his glasses. Or maybe she'd just imagined it.

"They like oranges in the West End," Amelia explained to Maisie as she handed a coin to the vendor.

"Give me nice ones," she told the vendor as he placed six oranges in her basket.

Amelia lifted one to her nose and inhaled.

"I love the smell," she said, her eyes closed. "Wonder what they taste like."

"They're good," Maisie said, hungry.

Amelia opened her eyes. "You've had one?"

Maisie nodded.

"Were you fancy before you entered the parish?" Amelia asked.

Maisie thought of Elm Medona and her pink pouf. She thought of the apartment on Bethune Street and all the Chinese dinners they'd eaten there.

"Yes," she said finally and sadly. "I was."

"Pity," Amelia said as they began to walk through Convent Garden and back to the street.

Suddenly, the smell of fresh-baked pies greeted Maisie. She took a big, deep breath, filling her nose with the smell of apples and berries.

But as they neared the pie men, she saw a small gaggle of people standing in front of them meowing.

"Meow!" they called to the pie men. "Meow!"

"I don't get it," Maisie said. "Why are they doing that?"

"It's the meat pies," Amelia said, wrinkling her nose. "Who knows what kind of meat is inside them? Meat is hard to come by, you know."

"But . . . are there *cats* in the pies?" Maisie asked in disbelief.

Amelia shrugged. "At the parish they put the dead children inside their pies. Who knows what this lot does?"

As they walked, Amelia pointed out what all the people scurrying about were doing.

"He's a dustman," she said. "Collects all the ashes and such from the dustbins."

The man was indeed covered with gray ash. It coated his hair, his clothes, his shoes. His eyes looked otherworldly peering out from all the dust around them.

"Coal porters," Amelia said as men wheeled small wheelbarrows of coal past them.

"Match girl," she said with obvious disgust. "Lower even than us, she is."

A small group of boys went past, each of them hauling a cloth bag over their shoulder.

"Rat catchers," Amelia said.

"What?" Maisie said, turning to take a look at the boys. Their bags were lumpy with . . . rats, she supposed, shivering.

"Here's our spot," Amelia said. "People come out of there"—she pointed to a brick building—"and they like a nice orange."

But people didn't come out. Not for a long while. Amelia didn't seem to mind the waiting. She called hello to some of the raggedy children who passed them. Children out in the street trying to make a half penny.

Maisie found her mind wandering back to Harrington Square and Grandfather Bell's nice warm house. She wondered how far it was from here to there. A light rain had started to fall, sending a chill through her. There would be a fire in the fireplace in the drawing room, Maisie knew. And hot tea with cake.

She took a good look at her surroundings. The police didn't seem to bother the street children during the day. As long as they were selling something or carrying packages or even doing cartwheels in the street, they seemed to be left alone. So she could probably make it back to Harrington Square without any trouble. But what would she do when night fell again? She thought of the garden across from the square. She could hide in there, couldn't she? Amongst the tall hedges maybe.

Besides, she had to get back to Aleck. He was the key to getting them out of this miserable city.

Them.

Her heart lurched at the idea of *them.* Hadley, her first real friend since they'd moved to Newport. Would she ever forgive Maisie for bringing her here and then losing her? And Rayne. Maisie didn't even know for sure that the sisters were together. Then the image of Felix hit her, his eyes beaming at her from behind his glasses, his cowlick popping up, his . . . oh, just his *Felix-ness.*

Where are you, Felix? Maisie thought.

⊃

"No way," Felix said, staring up into the long, narrow chimney. "I can't do it."

"You've no choice, mate," Johnny said. "Once you get inside, you'll feel the little spots where your feet can grip. You climb all the way to the top and—"

"No!" Felix said firmly.

Johnny gave him a little shove, sending him toppling forward.

"Climb," Johnny said evenly.

He blocked Felix's way with his body so that

there was just chimney in front of him and Johnny behind.

Felix took a deep breath and pulled himself inside the chimney. It was black in there. Black with soot and black with darkness. He looked up, but it was too dark to know how high it went.

"Climb!" Johnny yelled.

It was narrow. Felix wedged himself between the sides and pulled his way up a little, leaving his bare feet dangling free. He paused to catch his breath and think of a way out.

But the next thing he knew, Johnny was pricking the soles of his feet with pins, over and over.

Felix screamed. But he also shimmied up further, away from Johnny.

He paused again. The light from below seemed very far away now, and the darkness above seemed vast and endless.

Again, Johnny reached up and pricked his feet with the pins, piercing little stabs of pain that sent Felix up even more.

Felix felt hot tears on his cheeks. The soot was so thick he was having trouble catching his breath. Even though he knew it was silly, he closed his eyes.

Somehow the darkness there, behind his own eyes, was less scary.

"Sweep as you go!" Johnny called up to him.

Felix's foot found one of the small dents Johnny had told him he could use as a foothold. But when his toes moved to grip it, they slipped off, moist with sweat and blood.

Felix felt himself begin to slip.

Frantically he tried to push his shoulders against the sides of the chimney for support. His feet swung through the darkness, searching for another foothold.

But it was too late.

He was off-balance and falling.

His hands and cheeks scraped on the brick as he slid downward.

The light that had grown so far away now grew brighter and closer with increasing speed.

Felix heard his own voice making strangled, terrified sounds.

All of this happened in an instant, yet the fall seemed to go on forever.

Until finally Felix hit the bottom—hard.

He heard his glasses break.

He felt his head hit stone.

The taste of blood filled his mouth.

And then, like in cartoons he had seen, stars, pinpoints of light exploded in front of him. Then they extinguished and darkness followed. Felix felt himself slipping, slipping, slipping away.

"The sweep!" a woman in a haughty British accent shrieked. "He's dropped from the chimney."

Felix wanted to tell her that he wasn't a chimney sweep at all, but he felt as if he were falling again, this time into that darkness that enveloped him.

"Whatever shall I do?" the woman asked the empty cellar.

The last words that came into Felix's mind were *Eighteen Harrington Square.* But he couldn't remember what they meant, or why they were important.

That darkness finally covered him completely. And Felix did not hear or feel or think anything else.

CHAPTER 9

MRS. DUCKBERRY'S BRILLIANT IDEAS

Amelia's cheerfulness was getting on Maisie's nerves. Didn't the poor girl realize how bleak her life was? Maisie certainly did. They had stood on that corner all day trying to sell their measly six oranges. Most people who passed by pretended they didn't hear Amelia calling "*Oranges! Oranges for sale!*" A few looked at them with great pitiful faces and shook their heads sadly. But so far only one man had bought an orange.

Still, Amelia smiled prettily and called out "*Oranges! Oranges for sale!*" every time someone walked by, which was all the time. Maisie wished Amelia would shut up. She wished she could be somewhere warm and dry, with Felix and the Ziff twins. *Somewhere*, she thought sadly, *like Elm Medona.*

A fancy-looking woman, in a pale blue dress with so many petticoats beneath it that her bottom half swung to and fro like a big bell, hurried down the street. She carried so many packages that Maisie could only see her hat (also blue, though a darker shade than the dress), some curly brown bangs, and eyes peeking nervously over the smallest, highest package.

Of course it had started to rain, and the mud grew muddier. The woman had an umbrella hooked over her arm, but she had too many packages to reach it.

As she neared Maisie and Amelia, who quickly called "Oranges! Oranges for sale!" as if the woman could hold one more thing, her foot slipped in the slick mud and all of her packages went flying everywhere.

Maisie started to gather them, for they had been flung quite far from the woman, who miraculously remained standing.

"Oh dear!" the woman said, and stomped her foot.

She was wearing very peculiar-looking shoes.

Maisie handed her the packages she had retrieved,

helping to stack them from largest to smallest.

"There's one more, I'm afraid," the woman said apologetically. "A small square one?"

Maisie glanced around. Sure enough, a small square package lay upside down in the mud. She picked it up and wiped it off on her own filthy dress before setting it on the very top of the others.

Once again, the woman disappeared behind them, except her hat and bangs and her eyes which were—Maisie saw now that she stood so close to her—unusual. One eye was blue and the other green.

"It's these new pattens," the woman said. "They're slippery, which is silly since they're for walking through the mud, aren't they?"

Maisie surmised that *pattens* must be the peculiar things on the woman's feet, so she nodded.

"Want to buy an orange?" Amelia asked sweetly.

"Oh, dear, no," the woman said, not unkindly. "I have no money left at all after so much shopping."

A pained look flashed across her eyes.

"What a thoughtless thing to say!" the woman said. "I'm so sorry! Here you are, two children out on the street and I'm complaining . . ."

Her voice trailed off.

"I know!" she said suddenly. "You"—and here she directed her gaze at Maisie—"will come home with me so that I can give you a half penny for your help."

Before Maisie could answer, the woman said, "A half penny? No. I'll give you a pence."

Maisie could tell she was smiling behind her packages.

Another woman had stopped and was indeed buying one of Amelia's oranges.

But Maisie's woman had stepped to the street and hailed a taxi. Maisie hurried to open the door before the little boys lurking about did it, and then helped the woman and her packages into it. Without hesitating, Maisie got in, too. She didn't want the woman to change her mind.

"I love when I have a brilliant idea," the woman said happily, leaning back in the seat.

"So do I," Maisie said softly.

"Thank you for your help," the woman said. "I'm Mrs. William Duckberry."

She said this as if it might mean something to Maisie, but of course it didn't.

"Maisie Pickworth," Maisie introduced herself, deciding the name Pickworth sounded more impressive than Robbins. "Pleased to meet you."

The woman frowned. "Why, are you *American?*" she asked in disbelief.

Maisie nodded.

"Whatever is an *American* doing selling oranges on the streets of London?" she asked.

Maisie couldn't tell if this was a rhetorical question, but she decided to answer it.

"I came here with my brother and my friends, and we got separated and the police put me in a workhouse—"

"But where are your parents?" Mrs. Duckberry asked, horrified.

"Back in America," Maisie answered truthfully.

"This is most confusing," Mrs. Duckberry said, wrinkling her little button nose. "And most distressing! American children in a workhouse? Why, if President Lincoln ever heard we'd done such a thing he . . . he might start another war with us!"

Mrs. Duckberry, Maisie decided, might have been the prettiest woman she'd ever seen. Her skin was creamy and white. Her lips were pouty and pink. She had that button nose and dark brown ringlets and those mismatched eyes with long curly eyelashes.

"I must have another brilliant idea," Mrs. Duckberry said. She sighed, as if trying to conjure one.

After a few minutes of silence, Mrs. Duckberry brightened. "Aha!" she said. "You can stay with me until we straighten out this terrible mess. I'll wire your parents. Where did you say they were?"

"Um. Newport?"

"Rhode Island?" Mrs. Duckberry said. "Wait a minute . . . Pickworth? Is Phinneas Pickworth your father?"

Luckily, Mrs. Duckberry didn't wait for Maisie to answer, because Maisie was too shocked to say anything.

"I met him when I was there last summer," Mrs. Duckberry said. "What a character!" She shook her head fondly. "Well, I will wire him immediately and until he sends me instructions you will stay with me."

Satisfied, Mrs. Duckberry flashed a lovely smile at Maisie. But that smile turned quickly to a look of anxiety.

"We'll need to get you a bath and clothes, won't we? A workhouse! How absolutely terrible, you poor, poor girl."

With that, Mrs. Duckberry pulled Maisie to her bosom and hugged her hard. She smelled like perfume, but beneath the perfume she smelled kind of stinky. Maisie squirmed free.

"Mrs. Duckberry?" Maisie asked. "You're being so kind, but I wonder if I might ask a favor?"

"Anything!" Mrs. Duckberry said passionately. "Anything at all!"

"Can you help me find my brother and our friends?"

"Yes!" Mrs. Duckberry said triumphantly. "I can!"

There was a great deal of commotion on Mrs. Duckberry's street. Police huddled down at one end, where two men were carrying someone out of a house.

"What's the trouble?" Mrs. Duckberry asked one of the policemen as the cab slowed.

The policeman tipped his hat in her direction. "No trouble. A climbing boy fell, that's all."

"Poor, poor lad," Mrs. Duckberry said, motioning for the driver to continue. "I hope he's not dead," she added under her breath. "These poor suffering children."

Mrs. Duckberry's block was even fancier than

Grandfather Bell's. The houses stood taller and prettier and in front of them, behind ornate wrought iron gates, flowers bloomed.

"I'm so happy you're here," Mrs. Duckberry said to Maisie. "We're having a party tonight, and I just know you'll have a wonderful time."

Maisie made a move to start gathering the packages, but Mrs. Duckberry stopped her.

"Let that boy over there do it," she said, pointing to a little raggedy boy who was running toward the cab to open the door. "You're saved from labor now, Maisie."

Relieved, Maisie let the boy open the door for her and help her out. A look of confusion swept across his face when he saw Maisie in her own filthy clothes and bare feet.

"Don't stare," Mrs. Duckberry told him. "It's rude."

"Yes'm," the boy mumbled.

Maisie followed Mrs. Duckberry and her enormous bobbing skirt through the gate and up the stairs and into the house. Immediately a maid appeared, stopping short when she saw Maisie.

"This is Maisie Pickworth," Mrs. Duckberry

said. "An *American* lost in our terrible system, forced to work on the streets. Forced to walk *barefoot!* I'll wire her father immediately and until we get instructions you're to draw her a bath and find her suitable clothes."

As she spoke, Mrs. Duckberry removed her gloves and hat and deposited them in the maid's waiting hands.

Behind them came a clatter as the boy brought in the packages.

"Please get this boy a half penny," Mrs. Duckberry said to the maid.

She paused and looked at Maisie.

"Now Margaret will take very good care of you."

"Thank you," Maisie said.

Mrs. Duckworth headed for the winding staircase, but Maisie called to her.

"My brother?" Maisie reminded her. "Felix?"

Mrs. Duckworth slapped her forehead. "Of course, of course. And your friends. Tell me when you last saw them."

"Well, Felix was in the workhouse with me. I think he went off with a group called the sweeps?" Maisie offered.

"Oh no!" Mrs. Duckworth cried. "This is going to become an international incident! The sweeps? Are you sure, darling?"

"Pretty sure," Maisie said.

"Oh dear, *oh dear*, OH DEAR!"

"What are they?" Maisie asked. "The sweeps?"

"The queen herself will get involved if President Lincoln hears of this. An *American* sent off to be a sweep." Mrs. Duckberry shook her pretty head. "Dare I ask about the friends?"

"Hadley and Rayne Ziff," Maisie said. "The police were hauling us all off to that workhouse and . . . and . . ."

All of a sudden, Maisie realized just how terrible the situation was. Hadley and Rayne had vanished last night. And there were hundreds of children on the streets of London. Maybe thousands. How would anyone find Felix or the Ziff twins?

"Yes?" Mrs. Duckberry said gently.

"And they disappeared in the fog."

"Oh dear," Mrs. Duckberry said. "I have my work cut out for me. But don't you worry. I'll get a brilliant idea. I always do."

CHAPTER 10

DINNER WITH MR. DICKENS

Maisie could not believe how much she appreciated the pleasure of that hot bath. There had certainly been times, like after a softball game or an especially messy arts and crafts class, when a bath had been needed. But she had never been as dirty as she got in just twenty-four hours on the streets of London. Twice she had to get out of the oversize claw-foot tub, drain the water, and refill it because the bathwater had turned brown with mud.

Afterward, Maisie helped herself to some of Mrs. Duckberry's lavender water, which sat in a glass bottle on a shelf in the bathroom. The label on the bottle looked handwritten in black ink, the letters all curlicues and swirls. With such fancy scrolls, she could barely read what it said. But after she squinted at it long enough, she finally made out the words LAVENDER WATER and GIBSON'S APOTHECARY. Clearly that was where the stuff had come from, but Maisie still made a mental note to look up the word *apothecary* when she got home.

The maid had left out a long green dress with tiny mother-of-pearl buttons all the way down the front. Maisie ran her hands over the fine silk and smiled. She liked Mrs. Duckberry's fancy taste, Maisie decided. But then she saw the strange birdcage-like thing sitting beside it, and realized she was looking at the kind of device that made Mrs. Duckberry's skirt swing like a bell when she walked.

She picked the thing up. *Why in the world do women have to wear such ridiculous garments?* Maisie thought. All the men here strutted around in those tight pants and boots, like they were about to go off horseback riding. Their hair grew bushy and long, and they didn't even have to shave. But all day she'd stood on that street corner trying to sell oranges, and every woman who passed had on one of these ridiculous things, not to mention hats and gloves. *It certainly was better to be a man in Victorian England,*

Maisie thought as she tentatively stepped into the birdcage. In no time, she too swayed like a bell when she walked, feeling more ridiculous with every step she took.

⊃

With the bathing and the dressing and the considering of Victorian fashion, Maisie forgot for a while that she was alone and everyone else was lost on the streets of London. But as soon as she saw Mrs. Duckberry's worried face in the drawing room, she remembered her terrible predicament.

"Oh, darling, I am so sorry," Mrs. Duckberry said, wringing her lovely, soft hands. "It seems practically impossible to locate children out there. We simply have too many wandering about, poor things. One would think *American* children would be easier to find."

"You mean, they're lost for good?" Maisie said, horrified.

"We won't give up," Mrs. Duckberry said.

That was the kind of answer people gave when there was bad news, Maisie knew, and she felt tears spring to her eyes at the sound of Mrs. Duckberry's words.

"And brace yourself, Maisie," Mrs. Duckberry continued, "but it seems your father is traveling down the Nile and won't return for several weeks."

It took a moment for Maisie to realize that Mrs. Duckberry was talking about Phinneas Pickworth, and despite herself she smiled at the idea that he was her father.

"But we shan't give up," Mrs. Duckberry said again, patting Maisie's hand. "We'll find your brother and the Ziff sisters, and we'll get everyone back to Newport."

"Thank you," Maisie managed.

"In the meantime, we'll have a marvelous dinner party."

Mrs. Duckberry was interrupted by the maid coming in and handing her a silver tray with an envelope on it.

"Oh dear," Mrs. Duckberry said as she read the letter inside. "One of our guests is delayed. Seems he's had some unexpected guests of his own arrive and he's involved in his own practicalities."

Maisie watched as Mrs. Duckberry went to the small desk across the room, take out some paper and a fountain pen, dip the pen in an inkwell, and write a letter of her own. *How funny*, Maisie thought. *Before there were telephones, people who lived across town from each other had to communicate by writing letters.* No sooner did she have the thought, then her predicament came crashing back to her. Aleck was the person who was going to invent the telephone someday, and he was the person she needed to find again.

Felix had been right, Maisie thought. She never should have brought the Ziff twins into The Treasure Chest. Now she'd lost them. And Felix. And Aleck. So impossible did her situation seem at that instant that Maisie let out the biggest sigh of her life. She needed a brilliant idea, too. Fast.

By eight o'clock, Maisie's distress had faded to a dull ache in her chest. Almost a dozen fancy people filled Mrs. Duckberry's drawing room, sipping French wine and talking in their British accents. The swirl of velvet and smoke, of beards and ringlets, worked to distract Maisie from her troubles. She talked to Mrs. So and So (who also knew Phinneas Pickworth) about Newport and New York City, as if she, too, were a member of

high society. Most of the things Mrs. So and So
mentioned in those places were long gone, but
Maisie nodded and smiled as if they weren't, and
picked up a word of Mrs. So and So's in the process:
indeed. The way it worked was when Maisie had no
idea what someone was talking about, she smiled,
nodded, and said "Indeed." It seemed to mean yes,
no, *and* maybe.

Now Mrs. Someone Else was talking about the
poor street children of London. Unfortunately,
Maisie did know a little something about that
situation, but she chose to stick with what worked
best: Smile. Nod. "Indeed."

Mrs. Someone Else pointed her little pointy chin
in the direction of a dark-haired bearded man who
looked like all the other dark-haired bearded men.

"He knows something about it, doesn't he?" Mrs.
Someone Else said.

"Indeed," Maisie said, wondering if he ran one of
the workhouses or did something in government.

"Have you read them yet?" Mrs. Someone Else
asked.

Maisie nodded.

"Which ones?" Mrs. Someone Else continued.

She kept her eyes on the man, but Maisie knew she was talking to her.

This was the first question that one of Maisie's now practiced responses wouldn't answer.

Luckily Mrs. Someone Else liked the sound of her own voice so much that she answered her own question.

"I especially liked *David Copperfield*," she said.

"*David Copperfield*?" Maisie repeated. "I just saw that performed in Edinburgh."

"By him?" Mrs. Someone Else said, pointing her chin at the man again.

Maisie studied the man's face, on the off chance that Professor Bell was standing right in front of her at Mrs. Duckberry's house.

"No," she said finally.

The man turned then, as if he felt them staring.

"Mr. Dickens!" Mrs. Someone Else said, as if she'd just noticed him. "What a delightful surprise!"

To Maisie's delight, Charles Dickens smiled, nodded, and said "Indeed."

If there was one thing Maisie had learned since she'd moved to Elm Medona, it was that there were a lot of things she didn't know. However, even she—a mediocre reader and a bad historian—had heard of Charles Dickens

One Saturday between Thanksgiving and Christmas, her mother had taken Maisie and Felix to Providence to see *A Christmas Carol* at the Trinity Repertory Theater. Apparently they did the show every year.

"A holiday tradition!" their mother had said with forced cheerfulness, waving the tickets at Maisie and Felix.

Being their mother, of course they had to watch two different film versions of the story, too, one with Albert Finney as Scrooge and the other with George C. Scott. She even dug up a cartoon version with Mister Magoo playing Ebenezer Scrooge. Frankly, much to her mother's disappointment, that one was Maisie's favorite.

"I have a great idea," their mother had said. "We'll read the story out loud together! Won't that be special, sitting in the Reading Room and, well, reading?"

Maisie groaned. "Seriously?"

But Felix thought it was a great idea. He loved

the story, with the ghosts of Christmas Past, Present, and Future taking Scrooge through his life and showing him how sadly it would end if he didn't change his miserly ways.

"We could each read different parts," he proposed with so much excitement that Maisie groaned again.

Their mother's eyes looked bright. She grabbed a pad and pen and began to list all the characters.

"Let's see, I'll read Fen and Mrs. Cratchit and—"

"I want to be the Ghost of Christmas Present," Felix said. "And Tiny Tim!"

"Oh please," Maisie muttered. "Please let's not do this."

Luckily, their mother had to work late so many nights that the plan got waylaid. But thinking of how excited Felix had been about it made Maisie wish they had read the story out loud, that he had been able to be the Ghost of Christmas Present and Tiny Tim.

Even more, as she stood between Charles Dickens and Mrs. Someone Else, Maisie wished that Felix was here right this minute. He'd be able to say all kinds of smart things to Mr. Dickens. After all, he actually liked to read. And once he realized that they weren't all going to sit in the Reading Room every evening and read the thing out loud, he found a musty copy of it in the Library and read it himself.

Yes, Maisie thought as Mr. Dickens nodded and smiled at Mrs. Someone Else, *Felix should be here with me.*

Just as she had that thought, the maid appeared at the entrance to the drawing room and announced:

"Mrs. Duckberry, the Bells have arrived."

It took Maisie a moment to realize that the Bells were *her* Bells, Aleck and his grandfather.

And that with them, in dresses like the one Maisie wore, stood the Ziff twins.

⊃

At the same moment, Hadley realized that Maisie was standing gawking at her.

"Maisie!" she cried.

The two girls ran into each other's arms.

"What in the world happened to you?" Maisie managed to whisper.

"We got lost in that awful fog," Hadley said. "You have no idea what we had to do."

"Well, well, Aleck," Grandfather Bell said. "If it isn't your little friend."

Mrs. Duckberry clapped her hands in delight. "Now we have a real reason to celebrate," she said. "You're all reunited! Didn't I tell you it would work out, darling?"

"You mean Felix is here, too?" Rayne asked.

The adults in the room had all stopped talking, mesmerized by the three American girls' reunion.

"He isn't with you then?" Maisie asked.

Hadley shook her head no.

"If we found your friends," Mrs. Duckberry said optimistically, "then we will find Felix, too. Meanwhile, I have a beautiful lamb dinner about to be served in the dining room."

The guests took their cue and, chatting together again, moved into the dining room.

But Maisie and the Ziff twins hung back.

"It's been awful," Maisie told them. "We were taken to a workhouse, and I think Felix was sent out to clean chimneys."

"We met some children who earn money by raking the bottom of the Thames and selling what they find," Rayne said, her voice a mix of disgust and wonder.

"Oh, Maisie!" Hadley said. "I was so glad we had

our rain boots on! There was broken glass and nails everywhere—"

"But we did find a few pennies," Rayne added proudly.

Hadley opened the small ivory colored purse she had over her arm, carefully tugging its drawstrings and reaching inside.

"For you," she said to Maisie.

She opened her hand and dropped a quarter-size piece of milky-blue sea glass into Maisie's open palm.

"Technically," Hadley said, "I guess it's *river* glass."

"So pretty," Maisie said, holding it up so that the light from the gas lamp made it seem to glow.

None of the girls had noticed that Aleck stood in the doorway the entire time they talked. He stepped into the room now, clearing his throat with a big "*Ahem*" to announce his presence.

"I didn't mean to eavesdrop," he said when they looked up at him, surprised.

He didn't wait for them to respond.

"But this is a travesty," Aleck continued. "Four American children, working in the streets of London. Mudraking. Selling goods. Cleaning chimneys. Mr.

Dickens might very well put this in one of his novels."

"And Aleck," Maisie said, "Felix has disappeared. Even Mrs. Duckberry couldn't find him."

Aleck's eyes teared at her words. Maisie remembered how gently he'd pressed his lips to his mother's forehead when he spoke to her so that she could make out the words he was saying by feeling how his lips formed each one.

"You are a kind person, Alexander Graham Bell," Maisie said softly.

Aleck took Maisie's hands in his, and when he did she swooned ever so slightly.

"Maybe Grandfather can help," he said.

"Oh, Aleck. Do you think he would?" Maisie said.

"At least he'll try. I'm certain of that."

Now it was Rayne who *ahemed*.

"I think we need to join everyone at dinner," she said.

Awkwardly, Aleck released Maisie's hands.

"Yes, yes," he said, hurrying toward the door. "I think we should."

Hadley held Maisie back from following.

"How many girls can say that Alexander Graham

Bell has a crush on them?" she whispered. "This is a grand adventure, Maisie."

Usually Maisie would dispute a claim like that—she never thought a boy had a crush on her. But the way he'd turned his brown-eyed gaze on her, the way he'd held her hands and didn't let go . . .

"Yes," Maisie agreed, linking her arm in Hadley's. "This is a grand adventure."

Now if only they found Felix, it would be perfect.

⊃

"Just dreadful," an old woman named Mrs. Peacock was saying as Maisie slid into the seat beside her.

Mrs. Peacock had loose, wrinkly skin that trembled as she spoke. It was hard for Maisie not to stare at the folds of Mrs. Peacock's neck wiggling. Also, she wore so much face powder that Maisie could see the line beneath her chins where it stopped, and a perfect circle of very red rouge on each wrinkly cheek.

"The boy literally fell from the chimney onto the hard stone floor. Blood everywhere. Everywhere, I tell you," Mrs. Peacock said.

"He's lucky to be alive," Mrs. So and So said.

"Lucky?" Mrs. Somebody Else said, aghast. "He'll

be back in another chimney as soon as he's able. These children have no future. No hope. Isn't that correct, Mr. Dickens?"

"There's always hope," Grandfather Bell blurted out. "What we need is social reform—"

Mrs. Peacock leaned closer to Maisie, who had started picking at the slab of bloody lamb on her plate.

"The climbing boys have it the worst of the lot," she said in a stage whisper. "And this one was a new boy apparently. First day on the job."

"Possibly his last," Mrs. So and So butted in. "I mean, perhaps he'll be crippled now. Or worse."

Mrs. Peacock *tsked*. "The strangest thing of all," she said, her wrinkles shaking like mad, "is that it turns out the boy is an *American*."

"What?" Maisie, Hadley, Rayne, and Aleck said in unison.

Maisie got to her feet.

"Are you sure?" she asked Mrs. Peacock.

"Of course I'm sure. I saw him, didn't I? He landed in my basement, didn't he? He dropped from my chimney—"

"Where did they take him, Mrs. Peacock?" Mrs. Duckberry asked urgently.

"How would I know?" Mrs. Peacock said. "He isn't my responsibility, is he?"

Mr. Dickens shook his head, whether out of disgust or concern Maisie couldn't tell.

"A climbing boy?" he said in his deep voice. "They took him to the pauper's hospital in the East End, no doubt."

"Maisie," Aleck said, getting to his feet, too, now, "we'll go there right now. Grandfather, will your driver bring us?"

"Of course, of course."

"I just knew we'd find him," Mrs. Duckberry said to Maisie.

"Harrumph," Mrs. Peacock said. "Let's just hope the boy is still alive. That's all."

At that, Maisie gasped. "He has to be!" she said.

This time when Aleck took her hand, she was too upset to swoon. But she didn't let go either. That boy's large, warm hand was the one thing that made her feel safe as together they left the dining room and walked hurriedly to the front door.

CHAPTER 11

FINDING FELIX

A leck and Maisie sat quietly in the carriage as the driver moved through the fog and noise of London. Lost in her own thoughts and fears about Felix, Maisie didn't consider what might be on Aleck's mind until his soft voice said her name.

She looked toward him.

"Maisie," he said again, "I have a strange feeling . . ."

His voice trailed off and Maisie could tell that he was trying to sort something out.

"That magnet you gave me," Aleck said, and then once more his voice trailed off.

"Please," Maisie said, suddenly afraid that Aleck might say the very thing to her that would send them all hurtling back home. If Felix was injured, would he go with them? And if he did, what condition would he be in?

"Don't say anything," Maisie said urgently.

Bewildered, Aleck nodded. But an instant later he said, "I'm sorry, but I have to know something. Those coats and boots you were wearing, the . . . vinyl?"

It was Maisie's turn to nod now.

"And the magnet and . . . and . . . well, everything!" Aleck said, flustered. "The way you showed up in the park and then at our house—"

Maisie chewed her bottom lip, trying to decide what to tell him.

"Maisie," he said, his voice strong now, "are you from the future?"

Before she could answer, Aleck slapped his forehead.

"What an idiotic thing to say," he groaned.

"I am," Maisie said, surprising even herself. "All four of us are."

Maisie and Aleck stared at each other. Around them, the fog swirled and seemed to wrap itself around the carriage, obscuring everything outside.

"But how in the world—?" Aleck began.

"I'll try to explain it," Maisie said. "But you have to promise me something first."

"Anything," he said, sitting up straighter.

"Until we find Felix, you cannot tell me anything. Don't give me advice. Don't share any insight or information with me. Just listen to what I have to say and save your reactions until later."

"But how can I promise not to react?" Aleck said.

"That's the deal," Maisie told him firmly.

Aleck did not consider for long.

"All right," he said. "I promise."

Maisie told him about Elm Medona and Phinneas Pickworth, The Treasure Chest, and that first time they traveled and met Clara Barton. She told him about Great-Aunt Maisie and Great-Uncle Thorne, and *lame demon*, and the Ming vase shard. When she finished, she was breathless and Aleck's eyes were opened wide with wonder.

"How marvelous," he said quietly.

"I guess so," Maisie said. "Except when things go wrong, which they almost always do."

"Like now," Aleck added.

Maisie nodded.

"But how does it work?" Aleck asked, almost more to himself than to Maisie.

Maisie shrugged. "It seems like we learn something new every time."

"Like you're putting together a puzzle," Aleck said.

The carriage slowed and Maisie peered out the window into the foggy night. *Is Felix out there? Is he* . . . She squeezed her eyes shut, unable to imagine what was waiting for her in that hospital.

Aleck touched her shoulder.

"This is the East End," he said. "Grandfather warned me it's a tough part of the city, near the docks. Stay close to me, all right?"

The driver had walked around to open the carriage door, and as he did the smell of sewage and garbage filled the air.

Maisie's hand shot up to her nose and covered it.

"Stinking city," Aleck said. "Makes me homesick for Edinburgh."

The driver offered his hand to Maisie, and she stepped out of the carriage.

"Careful, Miss," the driver said. "I can't get any closer to the place."

For once, it wasn't raining. But still the road was muddy. There were no gas lamps here, and the dark seemed to stretch out forever. A shiver ran up Maisie's spine as she looked around and slowly followed Aleck toward the hospital

As soon as they were away from the carriage and halfway to the hospital, a gang of boys in various degrees of disarray—torn pants, torn shirts, bare feet, thin jackets, dirty faces and arms—surrounded them.

"Fancy," one of them said, giving a low whistle.

"You lost?" another asked Aleck, standing too close to him and then shoving him just a little.

"We're going in there," Aleck said.

"The pauper's hospital?" the boy said with a smirk.

"My brother's in there," Maisie said, hearing the desperation in her voice. "Please just let us go."

"Come on, you," a third boy said. He was the biggest of them all, and he towered above Maisie threateningly. "How would *your* brother be in there?"

"Yeah," said the dirtiest boy of all. "What you take us for? Fools?"

Maisie realized that the boys had formed a tight circle around her and Aleck, leaving no room for them to escape. The carriage and driver seemed to have vanished in the fog.

The boy who had shoved Aleck poked him in the chest.

"You sure don't look 'ungry, mate," he said.

"I don't have any money or food or anything," Aleck said. Maisie could tell he was struggling to keep calm.

"Sure you do," the boy said, poking him harder still. "Your lot always 'as something."

In a flash, the boys were on Aleck, knocking him to the ground and holding him there. He disappeared in a tangle of flying fists and bodies flung over him.

"Run!" Maisie heard him shout.

And run she did, calling "Help! Help!" as she did.

She thought she heard people laughing at her. Or was it just the wind? Lurching blindly forward, calling for help the whole way, Maisie moved toward a dull glow in the distance.

As she reached it, she could vaguely make out the image of a hulking gray building. Her foot smacked into something hard and she tripped, falling forward onto damp stone steps.

Hot tears sprung to her eyes as her shin hit the

edge. Instinctively, she reached down to touch it and felt a lump already forming.

Struggling to her feet, Maisie slowly felt her way up the stairs. The light there illuminated the double doors that led into the hospital. Through the glass, she could see nurses in long white uniforms with caps that looked like giant wings perched on their heads.

Maisie pounded on the door until one of them opened it.

At the sight of the nurse's kind, pale face, Maisie burst into tears. Behind her, Aleck was getting beat up; somewhere in here Felix lay helpless. She didn't know what to say first.

Through her muffled cries, she pointed behind her.

"Police," she managed to sputter.

The nurse's eyebrows shot upward and she reached for a long string, pulling it hard and sending a frantic bell ringing. Immediately, footsteps pounded down the corridor and two policemen appeared.

"My friend," Maisie gasped. "He's out there and these boys are beating him up—"

They didn't wait for her to finish. Sticks raised,

they rushed past her and out the door, shouting.

"You're bleeding," the nurse said kindly, pointing to Maisie's shin.

She took Maisie's arm and led her into a room that looked very much like a doctor's office.

"Let me clean that for you and bandage it," the nurse said.

Now that her tears had stopped and Maisie could see more clearly, she realized the nurse wasn't much older than she was.

"I'm Sally," the girl said.

"Maisie," Maisie said, through sniffles.

Sally took two steps backward.

"Maisie?" she repeated.

"Maisie Robbins," Maisie said.

"Thank the Lord," Sally said under her breath.

She began to clean Maisie's cut.

"I'll fix you up, and then I have something to show you," she said.

In no time, Sally was leading Maisie down the cold corridor. At the far end, she opened a door into a room lined with beds, just like the one at the workhouse. Except this place was clean and sterile looking, and it smelled like the iodine Maisie's father used to put on their skinned knees.

In each bed lay a boy who looked broken in some way. One had an arm in a stiff cast; the next had bandages around his head; another had both legs in the air, bandaged and attached to a big metal rod. Their faces were ashen, and here and there Maisie saw dried blood on a cheek or a chin or a forehead.

At last, Sally stopped.

She leaned over the figure that lay there. The boy had two black eyes and one side of his face was swollen and bruised. Beneath the bandages that were wrapped around his head, Maisie could make out jagged stitches and some dried blood.

Sally whispered, "I thought you was making her up, but she's here in the flesh. Your Maisie."

The boy's eyes fluttered open, and as soon as they did Maisie knew who this boy was.

"Felix," she said, sinking to the bed beside him with such relief that she couldn't say anything more.

"He's a lucky one," Sally was saying. "Two other climbing boys dropped today and they didn't make it. This one's been saying 'Maisie, Maisie, Maisie' every time he comes to. We thought he was delirious, what with the cracked skull and banged-up face. But here you are—Maisie."

Felix met Maisie's eyes and smiled.

"I knew you'd find me," he said. "I just knew it."

A loud racket erupted out in the hallway, and Sally ran to see what was happening.

"You were inside a chimney?" Maisie said to Felix.

He nodded. "Worse than when you jammed me in the dumbwaiter."

For the first time since she'd entered the room, Maisie became aware of all the groans and moans that filled it.

"Do you think you can leave here?" Maisie asked him.

His eyes filled with fear.

"I don't want to go back to that workhouse," he said.

"No, no," Maisie said soothingly. "I have a feeling that we'll be back home soon."

"What about Rayne and Hadley?"

"They're waiting for us," Maisie said.

Felix lifted himself up on his elbows. "What are you wearing?" he asked Maisie.

"I was at a dinner party," Maisie said, trying not to sound too braggy. After all, her poor brother had fallen down a chimney, cracked his head, broken his glasses, and lay here for hours and hours alone. She decided not to mention Charles Dickens. Yet.

Sally burst back into the room.

"Another boy saying 'Maisie, Maisie, Maisie'!" Sally said. "You've got boys all over London asking for you, don't you?"

Maisie jumped to her feet.

"Aleck!" she said. "I forgot all about him!"

"Stay put," Sally told her. "He's getting fixed up. Those hoodlums gave him some nasty scrapes and bruises."

"Aleck got beat up?" Felix said.

Sally shook her head sadly. "It's the East End," she said, "with all of our toughs."

When Aleck finally showed up, he looked even more shaken than Felix.

"Let's get out of here," he said.

"This boy needs rest," Sally told them, pointing to Felix. She handed him his broken glasses. "And some new spectacles."

Aleck and Maisie let Felix put an arm around each of their shoulders and they half-carried, half-walked him back outside to the carriage.

"Where were you?" Aleck asked the driver angrily. "We got attacked by a gang of boys."

"It was the fog," the driver said. "I was right over there but you couldn't even see me."

They all settled into the carriage, Maisie in the middle and the two boys each leaning on her ever so slightly.

Soon enough, Aleck spoke into the darkness.

"Do I do it?" he asked. "Do I find a way to make the deaf hear?"

Felix shot a look at Maisie, but she either ignored him or didn't see it.

"You find a way," Maisie said, "to let everyone hear."

They were silent again, with just the noise of London outside, and their own careful breathing inside.

"I miss Edinburgh," Aleck said finally. "I miss my parents and my brothers and even our old talking dog."

"Yes," Felix said, touching his sore cheek. "I'm ready to go home, too."

"But we need to leave, don't we?" Aleck said. "I believe this time away will change my life forever. I don't know how. But I believe it to be true. Maybe we can't appreciate the beauty of our hometown, or the love of our family, until we are thrust into a whole new world."

Felix wanted to agree, but he didn't have time.

In that instant, he was landing back in The Treasure Chest.

CHAPTER 12

RIVER GLASS

The four children lay in a tangled heap of arms and legs on the Oriental rug on The Treasure Chest floor.

"We're back," Hadley said, disappointed. "I was having the loveliest conversation with Mr. Dickens."

"What?" Felix demanded. "You met Charles Dickens? While I was getting myself knocked out . . ."

He paused.

His hand reached up to his face.

"My . . . my glasses," Felix said. "They're not broken."

Maisie was staring at her slicker and rain boots.

"And I'm not in that beautiful dress," she said.

"It's as if we weren't there at all," Rayne added sadly.

"But we were, weren't we?" Hadley asked.

"If it was a dream," Rayne decided, "then it was the loveliest dream ever."

Suddenly, the door to The Treasure Chest opened with a loud pop, and Great-Uncle Thorne marched in, waving a crowbar.

"How did you get in here?" he boomed. "One minute I'm feeling arthritic and tired, the next I have a bounce in my step."

He stopped and looked hard at the Ziff twins.

"And who are you two?" he boomed even louder.

Felix grinned at Great-Uncle Thorne.

"These are Amy Pickworth's great-great-grand daughters," he said.

Great-Uncle Thorne's face went pale. "But it can't be," he said.

"It's true!" Maisie said. "Amy married young, and her husband died before their baby was even born."

"Millicent," he said softly, nodding his head. "She was not raised a Pickworth. After Amy got lost in the Congo, her dead husband's family swooped in and took the child. No one ever saw or heard from her again."

Rayne and Hadley were nodding too.

"Millicent was our great-grandmother," Hadley said.

"My soul," Great-Uncle Thorne said, his voice tender. "More Pickworths."

He narrowed his eyes.

"So you all—" he began.

But he didn't have to finish. It was obvious that they had indeed all time traveled.

"Where?" he asked them gently.

"We were with Alexander Graham Bell," Maisie said.

Great-Uncle Thorne's eyes drifted across the objects in the room, alighting on one and then another and then another still.

"Maybe I won't seal the door again," he said, more to himself than to them. "Maybe I'll leave it open."

Distracted, he wandered away without another word to the children.

Hadley grabbed Maisie's arm.

"Our parents must be crazy with worry," she said. "I just realized we've been gone forever!"

"No," Felix told her. "Here, just a nanosecond has passed."

She looked at him dubiously.

"Look," he said, moving to the window. "It's still raining, right? And we left the window open, right?"

"Yes," Hadley said, considering.

"Well, there should be rain on the floor then, shouldn't there? If we've been gone as long as you think."

Hadley watched him as he swiped his hand across the floor.

"Practically dry," he announced.

"The thing is," Rayne said, "I want to go home and take a nice hot bath."

Hadley chimed in, "I want to smell the fresh air and give my parents a hug. Even though that was the most exciting experience I've ever had, I'm glad to be home."

"We have to leave home to appreciate it, I guess," Maisie said, thinking of Aleck. That was what he had told them, and that was the thing that sent them back. And after a night in that workhouse and that rainy day spent on the streets of London, even the servants' quarters sounded like a good enough home to Maisie.

"What have you two been up to?" Maisie and Felix's mother asked them that night after they suggested they all watch a movie together, whichever one she wanted.

"Oh, the usual," Maisie said.

"Yeah, just the usual," Felix added.

Their mother gave them a long, hard look.

"Why do I not believe you?" she said finally.

They both shrugged.

"*Hmmm*," she said. "Well, I'm going to take you up on your offer," she said.

"Great," Maisie said, meaning it.

"I'll make the popcorn," Felix volunteered. "I'll even put Parmesan cheese on it, just the way you like it."

"And I'll get a big blanket so we can all cuddle together and be nice and warm," Maisie said.

"Okay," their mother said, still studying them.

"Elm Medona," Felix said, "it feels like home."

"Even upstairs will be nice," Maisie added.

Their mother touched each of their foreheads.

"No fevers," she said. "I guess I'll just choose a movie and—"

"Anything but *Oliver!*" Maisie interrupted.

"Or *My Fair Lady*," Felix said.

"But anything else is okay," Maisie said.

"Okay," their mother said. "Oh, could you please hang up your wet raincoats before you come upstairs?"

Their mother wandered off to set up the DVD player, and Maisie and Felix went to hang up their raincoats.

"What in the world?" Maisie said when something fell out of her slicker's pocket.

Felix chased it across the floor and scooped it up.

"It looks like sea glass," he said.

Maisie looked at the pale green piece of glass he held out to her.

"River glass," she said.

She looked at her brother.

"It's from the Thames," she continued.

"You mean, it's from the past?" Felix asked her.

Maisie nodded.

"I didn't know we could take things back with us," Felix said.

Maisie closed her fingers around the smooth piece of glass.

"I have a feeling," she said, "that there's a lot we don't know about all of this."

If Felix and Maisie had been paying closer attention, they would have heard Great-Uncle Thorne, who stood hidden in the shadows, laugh ever so softly. They would have heard him say, "That's for certain."

Alexander Graham Bell

March 3, 1847 – August 2, 1922

Alexander Bell was born in Edinburgh, Scotland, and was named for both his father and grandfather. Both of his brothers had middle names, but he did not, so Aleck gave himself the middle name Graham when he was eleven years old. It was chosen to honor a close family friend.

His grandfather, uncle, and father were all elocutionists—teachers of speech—and his father's book on lip-reading for the deaf is still used today. Aleck did public exhibitions with his father to demonstrate Visible Speech. But Aleck was also influenced by his mother's deafness, which led him to study acoustics and sound.

Although he was a poor student, Aleck made his first invention when he was only twelve years old. One day, when he and his friend were playing in a grain mill, he watched the process of husking the wheat and decided it was too slow. Back at home, he built a device with rotating paddles that dehusked the wheat faster.

Soon after, his father took Aleck and his brother to see an automaton that simulated a human voice. Aleck was so impressed with what he saw that he convinced his older brother to help him build one of their own. Their father bought the materials for them to construct an artificial larynx, lips, and tongue, and eventually they succeeded in building an automaton that could say "Mama" when they forced air into its windpipe.

Excited by this first experiment with sound, Aleck then "taught" the family Skye terrier, Trouve, to talk by manipulating its vocal cords and lips with his hands. Soon afterward, he grew more serious and began using tuning forks and other devices to test the various aspects of sound and its transmission.

When Aleck was fifteen, he was sent to London to live with his grandfather for one year. It is widely believed that the playwright George Bernard Shaw wrote his play *Pygmalion* based on Aleck's grandfather's elocution work. *Pygmalion* was turned into the musical *My Fair Lady* in 1956. After the year with his grandfather, Aleck returned to Scotland, where he, too, began to teach elocution. A few years later, he moved to England with the rest of his family. But in just three short years, both of his brothers died. With Aleck sickly, too, his father believed that Canada was a healthier place to live, so Aleck moved there with his parents.

Eventually, he moved to Boston and taught at Boston University, where he continued his experiments in sound. Often, he would stay up all night and then teach all the next day. Finally he decided to give up teaching and work on his experiments instead. However he took on two private students as a source of income. One of them, Mabel Hubbard, who had been deaf since she was five years old, became Aleck's wife.

In 1864, telegraphs were one of the main forms of communication. The president of Western Union hired inventors Thomas Edison and Elisha Gray to find a way to send multiple messages on each telegraph line. At that time, Aleck was working on a method of sending multiple tones on a telegraph wire using a multi-reed device to be able to send a human voice over the telegraph wire.

On June 2, 1875, Bell's assistant, Thomas Watson, accidentally plucked one of the reeds. Bell heard the tones on his end of the wire, showing that multiple reeds were not necessary to transmit sound. Around the same time, Elisha Gray was experimenting with a water transmitter. On February 14, 1876, both Gray and Bell filed a patent for the first telephone, with

Bell beating Gray by allegedly just an hour. That short span of time made him the official inventor of the telephone.

Alexander Graham Bell spent his life inventing new things. His discoveries led to the invention of the phonograph, the iron lung (which helped people who could not breathe on their own), and a device for locating icebergs. And he never gave up his experiments with sound. Bell considered trying to impress a magnetic field on a record as a means of reproducing sound, but he ultimately abandoned the idea. That idea is the principle behind tape recorders and hard drives on computers. He also invented an early form of air conditioning, experimented with composting toilets, and considered using solar panels for heat.

In 1881, President James Garfield was shot, and the bullet was stuck inside his body. Bell was called in to try to find it. Bell quickly devised the first metal detector, but the doctor would not move the president from his metal bed, making detection impossible.

Alexander Graham Bell died at the age of seventy-five. On the day of his funeral, every telephone in North America was silenced for one hour in his honor.

Charles Dickens
February 7, 1812–June 9, 1870

The British novelist Charles Dickens is the author of many beloved classics such as *Oliver Twist*, which was adapted into the musical *Oliver!* that debuted in London in 1960 and was made into a film in 1968; *David Copperfield*, which Dickens based on his own life and was his favorite of his own novels; *A Tale of Two Cities*, which many consider to have one of the finest first lines ever written ("It was the best of times, it was the worst of times"); and *A Christmas Carol*, which features the miserly Ebenezer Scrooge who, with the help of three ghosts, finds the Christmas spirit. *A Christmas Carol* has been adapted for radio, film, stage, and television, including an animated version, *Mr. Magoo's Christmas Carol*. Quite an accomplishment for someone who had to leave school at the age of twelve and work in a shoe-polish factory to help support his family. His feelings of abandonment and betrayal of his parents became a major theme in his novels.

Alexander Graham Bell's father did indeed read

from the works of Charles Dickens in Edinburgh. Dickens himself toured the United States as a lecturer and was so popular that he is sometimes considered the first modern celebrity, earning over a million dollars in current US dollars. But he got his inspiration from the streets of Victorian London. When he died, at the age of fifty-eight, he was buried at Westminster Abbey and his funeral was attended by thousands of people.

ANN'S FAVORITE FACTS:

I do so much research for each book in The Treasure Chest series and discover so many cool facts that I can't fit into every book. Here are some of my favorites from my research for *The Treasure Chest: #7 Alexander Graham Bell: Master of Sound.* Enjoy!

When I was twelve, like Maisie and Felix are in the book, no one had cell phones. Instead, every telephone looked pretty much the same. Usually black, they were very heavy and had a big rotary dial. To make a call, you had to put your finger in the dial and spin it. There was no call waiting, so if the person you were calling was already talking to someone else, you got a busy signal—a loud beeping sound. No one had answering machines. If someone called while you were out, there was no way for you to know they'd called!

Turn the page for other facts about the telephone, including one that might surprise you:

Did Alexander Graham Bell really invent the telephone?

On March 7, 1876, Alexander Graham Bell was issued patent number 174,465 for an "improvement in telegraphy"—what became known as the telephone. Bell's patent was the fifth one registered at the patent office that day. A short time later, Elisha Gray, an inventor from Illinois who was also experimenting with transmitting sound across a single wire, filed a patent for "transmitting vocal sounds telegraphically." His was the thirty-ninth patent filed that day. The US Patent Office granted Bell's patent for the telephone because it was filed first, and forever after Alexander Graham Bell has been known as the inventor of the telephone.

The same year that Alexander Graham Bell made his first telephone call, Heinz ketchup was founded.

Alexander Graham Bell thought we should answer the phone "Hoy! Hoy!" instead of "Hello!"

In 1880, there were nearly fifty thousand phones in the United States. In 1980, there were 103,000,000.

Although we are used to picking up a telephone and calling anywhere in the world, it took time for service between cities to begin. The first telephone service established was in 1881 between Boston and Providence, RI. Service between New York and Chicago began in 1892. In 1894, service between New York and Boston started. On April 11, 1891, service began between London and Paris. But transcontinental United States service did not begin until 1915. And the first transatlantic cable was not available until 1956.

In the beginning, there were no telephone numbers. Instead, operators memorized the names and lines of all the subscribers. But a measles outbreak in Lowell, Massachusetts, led to a concern that the operators might miss work, and no one would be able to use their telephone. That's when the idea of telephone numbers was born.

The first telephone operators were actually young boys. Young boys had worked for low pay at telegraph offices, so everyone assumed they could easily work for telephone companies, too. But the boys didn't have the discipline needed to do the job of telephone operator. They made prank calls, grew impatient with the callers, and couldn't memorize the names and coordinating lines of subscribers. In 1878, the first female telephone operators were hired in Boston. Their pleasant voices and strong work ethic—as well as the fact that they could be paid low wages—made women perfect for the job, and soon all operators were female. By 1910, New York Telephone employed 6,000 female operators. But the first male telephone operator was not hired until the early 1970s, almost one hundred years later.

Bell Telephone was started in 1878 by Alexander Graham Bell with father-in-law, Gardiner Greene Hubbard, and a man named Thomas Samuels. The success of that company, which became AT&T, had much to do with Bell's future wife, Mabel Hubbard. Mabel thought Bell should show his invention at the 1876 US Centennial Exposition in Philadelphia. But the exposition ran during Bell's students' exam period. So Mabel secretly bought him a ticket from Boston to Philadelphia, packed his suitcase, and took him to the train station, where she revealed her plan. When Bell started to argue with her, Mabel, who had been deaf since she was five and relied on lip reading to "hear," simply looked away from him. It worked. Bell went to Philadelphia and displayed his telephone, which at first was met with indifference. But when Emperor Dom Pedro II of Brazil entered the Education Building and watched Bell demonstrate the telephone, he is said to have shouted: "My God! It talks!"—capturing the attention of the other visitors. Soon, people were lining up to talk to Bell over his telephone, and he won the Gold Medal for Electrical Equipment.

The writer Mark Twain was one of the first people to have a telephone in his home.

Most early residential telephones' numbers and lines were shared by two or more households. This was called a party line. The phone would ring in each house that shared that line. The conversation could be heard by everyone, and everyone could participate in it. Unique rings for each phone that shared a party line were developed to help with this. My aunt Angie had a party line even when I was a little girl. I used to love picking up her phone and eavesdropping on stranger's conversations!

The first pay telephone was installed in 1889. Calls were made by inserting coins into slots. Pay phones were popular everywhere until cell phones made them obsolete. The idea for cell phones came to a man named D. H. Ring in 1947, but the technology to make them did not yet exist. The first cell phone call, between an employee of AT&T and an employee of Motorola, happened in 1973. Japan was the first country to have a mobile phone network, in 1979.

The phrase "Put them on hold," actually comes from Bell handing Watson the telephone and saying, "Hold this," while he went to do something else.

Remember the rotary dial on my childhood telephone? That was invented in the late 1890s by Almon Brown Strowger. The first push-button phone wasn't invented until 1962. And today, there is one cell phone for every two people in the world. In the United States alone, there are more than three-hundred million cell phones.

Continue your adventures in The Treasure Chest!